A NOVEL BY
DOUG JOSEPH

I0543209

The Last Bye

BOOK THREE OF THE
SKYPORT CHRONICLES

WHITEST NE
PUBLISHING
STONEWOOD, WV, USA

The Last Bye
Book Three of the Skyport Chronicles
By Douglas G. Joseph

ISBN-10: 1628830069

ISBN-13: 978-1628830064

Library of Congress Control Number: 2013957501

MEET THE AUTHORS, WATCH VIDEOS & MORE AT
WHITESTONEPUBLISHING.COM
THE SOURCE FOR GREAT CHRISTIAN READING

WHITEST NE
PUBLISHING
CHRISTIAN RESOURCES | INSPIRATIONAL NOVELS | CHILDREN'S BOOKS

For Elliana, Kieran, Adena, and Gavin

CHAPTER 1

Split in Two

Gashed knuckles stung. Sweat poured. By the time the young runaway had finally climbed to the ledge that accessed the cave opening, his finger-tips, palms, and knees were raw and bleeding. Yet the fleshly wounds were eclipsed by the torment in his heart.

Due to P'erry's "sin curse" (that was his parents' term for it), the Corlan seemed to distrust him. He often felt despised and even hated by some, especially among the Corlan that were his own age. It did not start out that way, but his history of aggressive, loud-mouthed behavior had led to a very depressing state of affairs.

Now he so thoroughly hated his life on Sset that he did not know what to do. Ultimately, he just ran away. He had gathered some food and supplies along with a handful of belongings, and slipped away while no one was watching.

The ledge and cave were located high in a barren cliff face that overlooked the ocean. A flock of white moons dotted the sky. Thanks to the fiery glow-strip overhead (which spanned from horizon to horizon, splitting the blue sky in two), the daylight on Sset was somewhat brighter than on Earth, but that was totally normal for the boy. In fact, it was all he had ever known.

P'erry was not a native-born Corlan (his parents were originally from Earth, not Sset), but he had lived on the huge moon-world ever since birth. Regarding age, he was approaching his first *cam*. That would be like one's tenth birthday back on Earth, yet a cam is only one orbital "year" on Sset, because their world takes about ten times longer to orbit the gas giant, T'and, than our planet takes to orbit Sol, our sun.

As the boy had struggled toward the cave, due to his upward focus he had failed to notice that a massive population of *Tirra*—beautiful, winged creatures—had arrived far below him, skimming over the surface of the water. The highly intelligent beings were (regarding an Earth perspective) quite dragon-like, with an appearance resembling the giant pterosaurs of early Earth history.

When P'erry eventually turned to face the ocean, finally he saw the gathering of Tirra playfully swooping and soaring below. Part of him wanted to run back and tell everyone he had found them, but a flood of memories of being laughed to scorn in school (for suggesting out loud that they should locate the migrational Tirra and then fly on their backs to the New Land) made him want to lash out instead. It has been observed that when females of our kind are depressed they tend to retreat inward, whereas males tend to lash out when depressed.

As P'erry hung his head in despair, his eyes fell upon a heavy, sharp rock near his feet. He picked it up, and then looked with envy upon the innocent creatures playing in the air beneath him. Their sense of belonging, their care-free lives, their apparent joy and fun—it all offended him. He did not really know if they could carry a person on their backs or if they could fly as far as the New Land, but at that point he was so filled with a reciprocating hatred against the Corlan that he did not care.

As he lifted the rock to throw it toward a large batch of Tirra, he heard two voices shouting his name from some distance below. One was his father. The other was "Uncle Shao" (as his family called him). Shao was the oldest Corlan, the very first of a Human-like kind of people that were indigenous to the moon-world of Sset.

"P'erry! Stop!" his father shouted.

"P'erry! Don't throw that rock!" Uncle Shao yelled.

In a terrible moment of choice that seemed to last an eternity, P'erry willfully rebelled against the godly authority of his father and against the God-appointed leader of that world. As the rock left his bloody fingers, he immediately regretted the decision, and he began to hope the rock would miss the huge grouping of unaware beings below.

The rock fell a long way, and just before it landed in the water, it hit a young Tirra that looked barely old enough to fly. It was practically a baby. P'erry was not aiming for the baby, but he could not deny that he was trying to hit one of them deliberately. They were so thick —stacked up in different altitudes—that it would have been easier to hit one than to miss.

All was calm until the rock hit. The baby fell into the water, bleeding and motionless. It was hurt badly. The baby's mama saw it happen, and there was a long pause, while she glided motionlessly, as though she was in shock or denial. Then the mama Tirra went to her baby. She grabbed him with her back feet and carried him to the shore.

Then she went berserk. She started flying vertically, almost straight up toward P'erry. She was flapping hard and gaining altitude. Suddenly there was a race on between Shao (who was closer to P'erry than Daniel was) and the mama Tirra, both trying to reach P'erry. Shao seemed to sense that he might not be able to control the Tirra, and he was climbing to save the boy from her. Shao was much closer to the ledge than the mama, but the Tirra was ascending much more quickly than Shao could climb.

Shao was almost to the ledge when the mama Tirra flew past him. He called to her with an authority much like Adam must have had in the Garden of Eden before the fall of Humankind into sin.

"Stop!" Shao commanded loudly.

P'erry retreated back into the cave, as the mama Tirra landed on the ledge. She was breathing hard, and froth lined the back corners of her huge, beak-like mouth. She was so filled with fear and rage over the unprovoked attack against her family (perhaps even murder, if the baby should happen to not survive) that she was determined to retaliate, if for no other reason than to serve as judge, jury, and executioner to make sure that the wretched creature hiding from her in its evil lair would not be able to launch any such attacks ever again.

Her genuine fear of God and her respect for the man of God—Shao—caused her to pause. In a taut moment of choice that seemed to last an eternity, the mama Tirra deliberately yielded to and obeyed the authority of the God-appointed leader of her world.

P'erry was overcome with remorse, guilt, and fear, and he literally trembled and shook within the dark recess of the rock. Shao climbed onto the ledge, and then he spoke in the Corlan tongue directly to the enraged creature, as though he were addressing an equal.

"Please," Shao begged, "forgive this terrible trespass. The boy will be sorely punished. You have my word: this will never happen again! If your child dies, we will convene a meeting with your family and the Eldest of your kind to decide what to do. Let's not be rash. Please, let's go and tend to your cub right now."

The mother let out an awful sound that was a mix of agony, threat, and submission, as she dove off the ledge. P'erry's father, Daniel, finally made it to the ledge. It took only a glance from Shao to convey that he would go down to help the Tirra while Daniel should stay above with P'erry. It was very clear that P'erry's presence should not be forced on any of the Tirra at that moment in time.

Daniel sharply lamented, "Oh, how I wish that our teleportation skills worked in this universe!" Then he turned toward P'erry. "Son, what were you thinking?! What is going on in your brain? If that creature dies, there will be serious consequences, major repercussions."

P'erry just hung his head and sobbed uncontrollably. He could not find any words. He could not even breathe. Finally, his Daddy hugged him and said, "Come on, let's pray for God to work a miracle and save the baby's life."

They prayed together for God to spare the Tirra cub. When they finally climbed down from the cliff, P'erry's mother, *Tess*, had made it to their location. She scolded P'erry like only a mother can.

"P'erry Daniel Talbot! If you ever run away again, you'd better pray that we don't find you, or you'll be dead. And don't you ever throw a rock at anyone again, or I will feed you to the dragons myself!" That rebuke was before she calmed down and began to console him as she tried to get him to tell her what he was so upset about. He still could not find any words. She hugged him and held him. Finally she took time to notice the Tirra.

"Living, breathing, flying dragons," she whispered with awe.

"They're highly intelligent," Daniel observed. "Shao speaks to them just like you or me, and they understand him perfectly. They apparently have a society with appointed leaders or elders. They all have names, and they relate as families. I don't know exactly how they communicate, but clearly they have a language. It may or may not be Corlan, but obviously they can understand spoken Corlan quite easily."

P'erry asked, "So, they were called dragons on Earth?" He was hopeful for a chance to turn the conversation away from himself and his despicable actions that day.

His parents smiled at the sly maneuver. Daniel said, "Well, son, creatures similar to these once lived back on Earth, a long time before your mother and I were born. By the time we arrived, they had been extinct for a long while. All that was left of them were drawings, carvings, fossils, and stories, which were eventually embellished as legends and later dismissed by many as merely mythical."

P'erry studied the Tirra, still curious as to whether one of them could carry a person on his back in flight. He wondered how far they could fly, and whether or not they had ever found the New Land in their migrations.

Shao approached them and said, "The baby Tirra is named J'etsu. Learn his name, and remember it. P'erry, you must realize that we are not talking about some dumb animal of lower intelligence. He is a talking being. Just because he is not Corlan or Human does not mean that he is not a person. His people have laws, ethics, and great wisdom and understanding.

"J'etsu is not dead, but he has not yet regained consciousness. The bleeding is stopped, and the swelling is going down. His Tirran family is very thankful for our medical help. Really, I don't think it was our help that made the difference. It seems that the hand of the Lord is also at work, helping us. Nevertheless, the Tirra are crediting us for the improvement. That seems to be the Lord's intention."

Daniel touched Shao on the arm and said, "When we get back home, we will support you in an appropriate disciplinary action against P'erry."

Tess added her endorsement, "Yes, you will have our complete cooperation."

Shao leaned down and gathered P'erry's hands in his own, and said, "P'erry, you came here as an infant and saved the remnant of our people, the last thirteen of us, from certain death by taking our Corlan memories into yourself and stopping the Surati Plague. We will forever be thankful. However, your unwise choices and very destructive deeds today have resulted in a situation in which we have no choice but to discipline you. I wish that I could find a way to avoid it, but today I almost caused a conflict between their kind and our kind when I stopped the mama Tirra, *Jhatsu*, from attacking you. If we don't discipline you then it will sorely damage the peaceful relationship between our two peoples."

"I understand," P'erry said quietly.

Back at the settlement where the dwellings and other buildings were, P'erry was sent home to wait, and Daniel and *Tess* talked in an outer chamber while the eight Corlan adults discussed the matter in a private gathering.

Daniel paced the floor as he vented aloud, "You know, back when the Lord first sent us here, I was all up for the adventure of our baby saving the Corlan. I'm still trusting in Him, but things are getting very complicated for P'erry. Let's review what we know.

"P'erry is not allowed back on the New Earth, because he was made under the sin curse. The Lord has let us know that we're supposed to stay here on Sset for P'erry's whole life. Unlike normal parents, we know for certain we will see the death of our son, not the other way around. His only shot at a good life is here on Sset with the Corlan.

"The five Corlan kids are getting inherited memories transcribed in batches every night. P'erry's getting none, even though the surati microbes were implanted in him right at the start. The Corlan have noticed that he is not getting any memories. They can deal with the fact that he has no belly button—Shao is like that; neither the husband nor the wife has a belly button. But some are having trouble with the fact that he is not getting any memories. They've also been plagued by his orneriness and his moodiness. They don't ever act like that. Never have. When he acts that way, it frightens them.

"What's more, the Corlan kids are an odd number. When they eventually pair off to get married, one girl will have no husband, unless she marries P'erry, a sin-cursed Human, instead of a Corlan. But wait—that's no real problem, 'cause she can just wait a while longer and marry one of her second cousins. Her people have been using that option for generations if someone of their own age didn't suit their fancy. Their gene pool is so pure that it makes no difference whether they marry a near sibling, a first cousin, or a second cousin. They—"

Tess interrupted, "But Dan, they've already paired off. Two days ago Karq's boy, T'anah, got engaged to *Z'aey*, Swov's orphaned granddaughter. And then just yesterday Swov's son, R'ei, announced that he is betrothed to Tap's daughter, *B'rei*. The only two kids who are not spoken for are Shao's daughter, *C'lou*, and our son. A Corlan and a Human."

Daniel opened his mouth in shock and said, "What?!

They've already paired off—at not even one cam of age? That's like not even ten years old, in Earth time! They have eleven more cam to wait before they can mate! I guess I've been so involved with the irrigation work I missed all this."

"I know!" *Tess* replied. "Even by Corlan standards this is a very early pairing. I'm guessing that, deep down, none of the Corlan girls wants to marry a mortal, sin-cursed Human husband, and so the heat is on. Either that, or perhaps their parents don't want to see it happen. Or both. Either way, someone has been putting on the pressure for them to pair up sooner rather than later. It's like a game of musical chairs, only the last one standing has to either marry our son, or else wait 12 more cam for a Corlan spouse that's a second cousin, and then wait just as long again before they can mate with their Corlan second cousin. And that's assuming we've somehow made it to the New Land before then, or else none of them will still be alive after eating this contaminated plant life for that long. The damages of their own Surati Plague are still in force, yet P'erry is taking flak for being sin cursed."

Daniel stopped pacing and said, "Now I see. The fact that everybody is paired up except for *C'lou* and P'erry, has caused him to feel rejected and scorned. He feels too insecure to ask *C'lou* to marry him—who wouldn't, at ten years of age, especially in his position—and he feels ashamed that everyone else is already spoken for. *C'lou* won't approach him. In fact, she can't. For her to ask him to marry her would be against Corlan tradition."

Tess said, "If I were in his place, at his age, I probably would have run away too."

Shao was still addressing the Corlan adults inside the private meeting room.

"Clearly the boy's Human nature would be behind such an act," he said. "Nevertheless, we must bear in mind that it was a Corlan's sinfulness, not Human, that led to the Surati Plague. The wicked Ettosedondi's terrible deeds jeopardized us all, and we would have died a cam ago if it were not for this Human, P'erry. Furthermore, need I remind you that the Lord has revealed to me that P'erry will be the key to our successful journey to the New Land? The inert surati powder left over after the plague has contaminated all the plants that we have reseeded. Because of the Ettosedondi, we have had to split our seed stores in two. We must protect the uncorrupted half until we get to the New Land that has been promised to us. We need P'erry's help if we are to get there. We must convince the Tirra of as light a punishment as we can get away with. We need P'erry on our side. We must have P'erry on our side.

"Speaking of which, this recent business of extremely early betrothals seems to have pushed the boy into despair. Put yourself in his place. He is utterly humiliated. I dare say that any of us, if we found ourselves under the same burden and circumstances, would have behaved the same. We may have unwittingly caused this ordeal by allowing our children to behave as they have.

"I cannot demand of any of you to compel your child to be wedded to a sin-cursed Human, but there is some good in him, if you will look to see it. If he is ever to be found pleasing in God's eyes, we must help his parents win his soul over to the right side, the side of truth. It is difficult for us to comprehend, this Human condition of being lost and needing to be found, but that was the way of things on their world.

"Back on Earth—which is a place where he cannot now go—they used to have a thing called being 'born again,' a type of conversion experience in which a sin-cursed Human would turn away from the evil side of their nature, and go through a water-covering ceremony in the Lord's name given in their Earth tongue, and become 'filled' with the same precious Spirit of God by which we fellowship with Him every day. The experience regenerated them and changed them. It made them more like us. It gave them the chance to become more like a Corlan. This is what we need to see happen. We need for P'erry to undergo this conversion experience, and become Corlan. We need him to become one of us. The keystone of this adoption is whether you and I will ever truly adopt him into our family. We must be willing to view him as truly Corlan when that time comes."

Karq (the husband), the one who often questioned and occasionally objected, spoke up, "But, Sire, what of the fact that he is not getting any of the memories? Can he ever be truly Corlan without getting the memories?"

Shao replied, "I am Corlan, and I never had a single memory given to me by my surati. I gave them my memories, but I never received memories from them. I got all my memories in a way that is quite Human. I lived new experiences and gained all the memories. The same is true of my wife, your First Mother. She never received memories, only gave them.

"Perhaps it is good that P'erry, like my wife and me, had no umbilical cord and therefore has no navel. Perhaps he is, in a way, the second Shao, a new Corlan who will get his wisdom only by living the experiences and earning the memories. I pray it is so."

Tap stood and offered, "Let us pray, and if it seems good to the Lord, and to all of us, then let us tell P'erry's parents that we will trust them to discipline their son as they see fit. If the Tirran child had died, we would have no choice but to intervene. However, since the child survived, perhaps we can allow the discipline to be the parents' duty and responsibility. We would tell them that we support them, and then we would report to the Tirra that sufficient measures were taken."

Shao nodded a glowing approval. Prayer was made,

and the Lord signaled His approval to all of them. Shao verbally confirmed this, and no objections were offered. They called for Daniel and *Tess* to come in.

When the two glorified immortals entered the room, *Swov* (the wife), who had much wisdom, addressed them, "Your precious son and our precious home world have much in common. Both are split in two. Our plant seed is divided in two. Half is for planting in contaminated soil. Half is for planting in uncorrupted soil. This continent is forever spoiled, and we must leave it. A promised land across the ocean awaits us, a continent where there is no contamination. There we must go.

"Yet we cannot get there on our own. You know this, as you sailed with us by ship, two denicam ago, when we tried to journey there by our own efforts. You know how that mission failed. We could not find the New Land, and eventually we had to confess that our own skill could not bring success. Had we not turned back, we would have starved to death on the open sea. The Lord has shown through our Eldest that we need P'erry for the mission. He is the key. Somehow he will get us there.

"Similar to our corrupted continent, P'erry's very nature is contaminated. Like us, he needs to abandon his corrupt state and gain an uncorrupted nature. Like us, he cannot make that journey without outside help, no matter how much he may desire it. Just as we need his help, and the Lord's help through him, he needs our help, and the Lord's help through us.

"We pledge to you this help. As P'erry will one day help us to gain life on the pure continent, we pledge to help him to one day become the pure, uncorrupted P'erry that we all hope to see. Both his journey and ours can only succeed by God's help. We know that, as a Human, P'erry needs to have a conversion experience, and we believe that somehow it is the necessary first step. Please forgive us for failing to help you win him to truth. Please forgive us for allowing our children to do things that resulted in humiliating him. We will do better."

Her husband then added, "As a matter of fact, we are now going to ask for something that has never been done in Corlan history. We would like to ask Tap if they would agree with us regarding the annulment of the very early betrothal of our son to their daughter, and we would like to express to Karq that we are open to such a request regarding T'anah's engagement to *Z'aey*. Corlan engagements have never occurred so early, and we have not felt comfortable about it."

Tap, both the husband and wife, nodded in agreement.

Tap (the wife) said, "If, later on, they decide to redo the agreement (when they are older and the time is right) that will be permissible, but I agree that the engagement needs to be annulled for now."

Tap (the husband) nodded firmly in agreement. They also had been very uncomfortable about the ultra early betrothals.

No one in the room turned toward Karq, but there was a reasonable hope that both he and she would request the same action. They both fidgeted in their seats while glancing at one another. When the silence became unbearable, they ever so reluctantly requested to have their son's engagement to Swov's orphaned granddaughter, *Z'aey*, annulled. At that point, there was little doubt about the source for the majority of the pressure for the early betrothals.

Shao addressed the Talbots, "We have decided to leave in your hands the question of what discipline P'erry needs. We will trust you completely, and we will defend your decision to the Tirra. We have prayed and we have confirmation in the Spirit that this is acceptable to the Lord. It is our goal for P'erry to truly be accepted as Corlan and for him to know in his heart that he is one of us."

Daniel and *Tess* both offered a series of thank-you statements, and they returned to their home relieved, thankful, and impressed with the wisdom of the Corlan people. Both of them had noticed the awkwardness of the situation with Karq, and they decided that it was an acceptable imperfection in an otherwise overwhelming effort to accommodate their difficult situation.

They set their attention to deciding on a suitable discipline for P'erry's actions. They settled on a spanking of five lashes (the most they had ever given), in addition to a quarter of a denicam (about three months in Earth time) during which P'erry was to have no access to his rock collection, no exploration or adventure, and he was to double up on his hours spent helping the men with the irrigation project. This was to be in addition to regular schooling, which was to proceed as normal. P'erry was fine with all of it except the schooling. He dreaded going to class.

After administering the spanking, Daniel hugged P'erry closely and said, "Son, I love you, but you have got to straighten up. Do you understand?"

"Yes, sir," he replied. Then he pleaded, "But Dad, can't we make it so that a time away from school will be part of my punishment? I hate going to school with them. They don't like me. They're all smarter than me, and the more memories they get, the smarter they are. They all get new Corlan memories every night, and I always get none."

"No, son. The desire of the Corlan adults is to accept you as truly Corlan, not just as a Human interloper. They are working to get their kids to see the wisdom in this. They are right about this. It's the right thing to do. If we were to pull you out of school right now, it would be counterproductive. It would work against what everyone is trying to do. Besides, I think you will find that the others will treat you differently from now on. I hope."

"I know one kid who won't," P'erry sullenly declared.

"Who?"

"T'anah."

T'anah, Karq's son, was "obviously" handsome, with blue eyes, a finely chiseled nose, strong chin and generally prominent features topped off with blondish hair. He was smart and funny, and he seemed like a natural leader. Yet P'erry perceived T'anah as a bit snobbish, somewhat arrogant. He had good reason.

Besides T'anah and P'erry, there was only one other boy on all of Sset (there were only two Corlan boys whose families survived the Surati Plague). The other boy's name was R'ei. He was Swov's son. R'ei was "ruggedly" handsome, with dark, brooding eyes, black hair, and an oval face that tapered to a narrow chin.

P'erry felt "plain" looking in comparison to either T'anah or R'ei. His straight bangs of brown hair hovered over hazel eyes that always seemed angry. His mouth, which would otherwise have been quite handsome, was often pursed in a tense half-frown. Lately he was generally unhappy, and everyone knew it.

At school in the days afterward, the adult teachers (Swov, both husband and wife) and all the Corlan kids acted in a way that seemed more sensitive to P'erry's situation and dilemma. Even T'anah seemed more kind, at least in front of the adults. Yet privately he was somewhat different.

At one point, T'anah pulled him aside in the hallway

and said, "Listen, P'erry, I admit that your 'sin-curse' frightens me, and that I have treated you poorly because of it. However, even you have to admit that having our parents break up my betrothal to *Z'aey* was going too far. Truthfully, I am still bothered by you, and I am just doing my best to please everyone else. They say that a sin-cursed Human can get God to change them. If you're going to do that, I wish you would go ahead. Until then you frustrate me, and I don't like it. I'm just being honest. I still don't care for you at all."

P'erry responded in a way that many a red-blooded, unredeemed, ten-year-old Earth boy would have responded. He just punched T'anah in the nose.

T'anah just shook his head, grabbed his nose, and quickly walked away. Several times during their early childhood, P'erry had pulled stunts the likes of which the Corlan kids never did (including biting, hitting, kicking, and so on). It was a big part of why the Corlan struggled to even understand him, let alone love him. In those instances, none of the Corlan kids ever retaliated. They always just took it and walked away, yet it only made things harder for P'erry in the long run.

A trail of blood drops on the stone floor betrayed to Swov that once again something had gone terribly wrong. After investigating, he simply wrote out yet another note of explanation, handed it to P'erry, and sent him home. P'erry would receive yet another spanking from his parents. His level of frustration had not changed much.

The Corlan delegation to the Tirra returned with a mixed report. Shao explained the details to everyone at that evening's gathering.

"The Tirra accepted the news about P'erry's punishment without comment, at first," he said. "Then later they stipulated that P'erry is not to be permitted in the areas of their migration homes. When we offered P'erry's plea of repentance and asked about forgiveness, we were told that it is their judgment in this instance that only the victim could request a proceeding toward forgiveness and reconciliation, and that only the victim could grant that forgiveness. At the present time, J'etsu is not interested in any dialogue with P'erry, whom they deem to be a creature of darkness."

THE LAST BYE

CHAPTER II

A New Hope

Every evening the Corlan had a wonderful time of fellowship and worship to the Lord. It was a very liberated and informal time of what would be called "church" back on Earth. Then each Densed (each "tenth day") there was an all-out "church party" with dancing in the Spirit, music, food, fun, games, and times of family relaxation. (The Lord created the Corlan cyntu, or universe, in nine days, not six, and so their day of rest comes every tenth day, instead of every seventh day.)

The Corlan had never had to atone for anything significant, and their relationship with the Lord was still rather innocent. So their "church" gathering had never needed an altar call or an altar. Daniel spent some time trying to explain to them why P'erry needed something more than they were used to. They tried to understand, but the concept was alien to them and it flubbed pretty badly. There was a period of giving "altar calls" during which P'erry was too embarrassed to be singled out, even if he had wanted to pray or repent or ask God for His Spirit, and he was not sure that he wanted to do such things in the first place. Daniel and *Tess* could clearly see that it was not working, so they told Shao, who had the Corlan to abandon that approach. It was decided that they would just have to give P'erry a chance to mature and to reach out to the Lord in his own way and in his own timing.

Somehow P'erry managed to sweat out four more denicam of schooling. He turned 1.4 cam of age (the equivalent of about 14 years in Earth time). He was then a little more mature, and had finally stopped the childish practices of hitting and kicking, etc. He still had a lot of bitterness though. He basically went through his days with a chip on his shoulder. One day after school, Shao's daughter, *C'lou*, told him something that changed his outlook dramatically.

While no one else was listening, she said to him, "You know, P'erry, all three of us girls think you are nice looking. It's just that your personality needs major improvement. You have brought onto yourself most of the troubles that you face. If you would not carry such a bitter attitude, you would find things much easier. My father says that if you would ever be 'born again' then none of us girls should think that marrying you is out of the question, even if you don't live forever after we get to the New Land. I'll tell you a secret. I like you a little bit. But my Dad says I'm not allowed to like you at all unless you have this 'conversion experience' first. So… anyway, just wanted to say that."

Then she turned and walked on homeward. P'erry just smiled a giddy smile and then floated home in a daze. He could not have been more shocked if she had kissed him. He never dreamed that any of the beautiful Corlan girls would ever pay him any attention (not any positive attention, that is).

All three of the Corlan girls, *C'lou*, *B'rei*, and *Z'aey*, had light colored hair, but *C'lou's* was a sandy, brownish blond while the other two were brighter, lighter blonds. None of the kids, boy or girl, had yet experienced c'ali (puberty), but anyone could tell that these three girls were going to become very beautiful ladies.

They were all extremely intelligent, and both *C'lou* and *B'rei* were of very sweet dispositions. *Z'aey* was doing her best to deal with growing up as an adopted orphan. She was not that awfully unpleasant. She just suffered a sense of loss and battled feelings of self-pity. She could at times act like she had a chip on her shoulder. One might have thought that she and P'erry would therefore have something in common, but she actually seemed to gravitate more toward T'anah's personality and way of thinking.

Once at home, P'erry asked, "Mom, where's Dad?"

"He is out helping with the irrigation. The Surati Plague did a lot of damage as far as soil erosion goes. Who knows how long he will be working on it?" As always, she was working on her genetic study of the tainted Corlan food plants.

"Can I go and find him? I need to ask him something."

"Yes, honey," she said. After he walked out, she stopped her research and stared out after him. He had never acted this way before. She could not put her finger on what was different, but something in his tone....

P'erry found his father, and asked, "Dad, can I talk to you?"

"Sure."

"How long do you think I will live?"

"Well, son, that's a good question. Any particular reason you're asking?"

"Just now, *C'lou* said something that staggered me. I always assumed I was destined to live and die without a wife. Today she told me that she likes me, kind of, and that if I would be born again and let God change me, she was not opposed to marrying me. Even her father is not opposed to it. Uncle Shao told her that any of the Corlan girls should be willing to marry me, if I let the Lord change me through the conversion experience, even if I cannot live forever once we all get to the New Land."

"Wow."

"This changes everything, Dad!"

"No doubt!"

"So now I want to know, how long will I live?"

"Well son, assuming that you don't get yourself killed first by an angry Tirran mama dragon… a Human being has the genetic potential to live a long time, given the right conditions—possibly even forever with perfect conditions such as once existed in the Garden of Eden. Back on Earth, in the early days after the fall of man into the sin curse, some people lived almost a thousand years, which would be about a hundred cam.

"Here on Sset, the atmosphere is at a higher pressure than on the post-flood Earth, and the air here contains a higher percentage of oxygen. The food here, even the contaminated food, is much better for people than what was on Earth after the fall, especially after the flood of Noah's day. So, I would say you could easily live a hundred cam, maybe much longer.

"The wild card here is the contaminated food. With eating it, perhaps your lifespan will be much less, maybe seven, ten, or twelve cam. With eating pure food, it would no doubt be much longer. And I could be way off. It might be a hundred cam with contaminated food, and a thousand cam with pure food.

"If you had lived back on the Old Earth with us, before the Rapture, you would already be experiencing your c'ali by now, which we called puberty back then. The fact that you are not yet having any outward signs means clearly you are already set to live longer here than you would have on the Earth, which would have been about seven or eight cam."

"Signs? What signs?"

"Well, do you see how the adult men have facial hair? That's one outward sign. There are other signs that are similar. There are also a lot of inward changes too."

"Do you think I will have my c'ali at the same time as the Corlan kids?"

"I hope so! For your sake."

They had talked the whole way home. When they arrived, *Tess* was bubbling over about her research breakthrough.

"I have proved that the contamination altered the very DNA of the plants, and that the alteration can be spread through pollination!"

"Excellent work!" Daniel said, "I had known that some parts of Human DNA could be partially rewritten, even after conception, based on one's circumstances. That was proven a long time ago back on Earth, but I never realized we could be dealing with that in plants too. What exactly does this mean for us?"

"It means several things. One, it pretty much means we *must* get to the New Land. We already knew that, but this underscores it. Trying to get around the problem while still here is a lost cause. Even with a hermetically sealed greenhouse environment, it would be impossible to totally protect against any outside pollen, unless we all lived inside it. As the population grows, that would become impossible. Not to mention the impossible task of finding enough soil that does not contain any of the inert surati that can re-cause the problem to begin with.

"Furthermore, it means that even if we *had* discovered the other continent via the ship on our first voyage, we might have contaminated it, because we did not know to screen for pollen. Even a small amount on our bodies, boxes, or food stores, could have recreated the problem in the New Land. In the same way that the ancient Jews cleaned all of the leaven out of their houses for the Passover, we are going to have to clean away every bit of pollen for our journey into the Promised Land.

"This is obvious, but if God planned to simply work a miracle to stop the problem, He would never have told them to go to the New Land. Finally, since God already foresaw all of this, I'm guessing the New Land is very far away, or else there could be a transfer of the contaminant pollen via transoceanic winds or the migrations of animal life. That poses some interesting questions for us about the ocean voyage being longer than we originally hoped."

"Ouch," Daniel said. "Besides the two of us, no one else would be able to survive a longer ocean trip unless we build a much bigger boat and take a much larger supply of food."

After a brief pause, *Tess* said, "P'erry's different today, but in a good way. He has not yet told me why. Are you in the loop?"

"Well," Daniel said, "I will let him tell you. It's about a *girl!*"

"Dad!" P'erry wailed.

"What!?" Tess demanded. She was elated and shocked.

P'erry shook his head as he blushed, and then he said, "*C'lou* told me she likes me a little bit, but she is not allowed to really like me unless I get born again. Another huge deal is that her father is not opposed to her marrying me."

"As long as you turn your life around and serve the Lord," *Tess* added.

"Right."

Tess said, "Listen to your mother. Getting into church just to get a girl is the wrong reason. It is not fair to God, the girl, or yourself. If you decide to serve God, it'd better be for real, with your whole heart. Do you hear me?"

"Yes, ma'am," P'erry acknowledged. He then slowly made his way to his room.

Later on, during dinner, all he said about the matter was, "Do you think there is any chance the Lord will let me live forever in the New Land?"

"No and yes," Daniel said. "No, I don't think He will let you live forever anywhere in your current body. The general rule for sin-cursed Humans is 'it is appointed unto men once to die, but after this the judgment.' Nevertheless, yes, I think He will let you live forever wherever you want, in a glorified, immortal body, like ours, if you serve Him with your whole heart, and let Him help you."

P'erry then asked, "If I serve Him, and I eventually get a glorified body here on Sset, do you think I will be able to teleport in this cyntu, just like you can in your old cyntu?"

"Possibly. Maybe. And you never know, you just might be able to teach us old dogs a new trick. We may one day learn how to teleport here."

P'erry quizzed, "What does 'teach us old dogs a new trick' mean?"

"It's just an old saying, from back on Earth. A dog is an animal, sort of like a teg here on Sset, but smarter."

P'erry wondered what kind of "tricks" a teg could be taught. He could not think of anything that would be worth the time or trouble.

"My parents with their crazy Earth history," he said. "What funny stuff you did back then!"

His parents laughed, and Daniel tousled his son's hair.

Daniel said, "Come on, we all need to go tell Shao what your Mom has discovered."

P'erry suddenly got very nervous.

"No, Dad," he begged, "you go without me. I don't think I could look Uncle Shao in the eyes after what *C'lou* said to me today."

"You mean you don't want to go see your new *girl-friend?*" his mother teased.

"Mom!" he yelled. "She's not my girlfriend."

"How so?" she asked. "She likes you, and she's a girl. Sounds like a *girlfriend* to me."

"This is hopeless!" he lamented, yet in a good humor with well-intended sarcasm.

In the end he did go, but he tried to make himself scarce. He said practically nothing. He was both relieved and disappointed that *C'lou* was not home at the time of their visit. She had gone somewhere with her mother.

Shao and Daniel talked of the great sacrifice it took previously for everyone to build the modest sailing ship that they had used on their first voyage. Prior to the Surati Plague, the Corlan had not built large sea vessels. Neither Daniel nor *Tess* was an expert at sailing, but they held just enough memories from their time on Earth to guide the Corlan in the general principles of sailing.

The two men spoke with trepidation about the massive task of building a ship that would be twice as large as the first one. They also considered the challenges of gathering enough food to fill it and the logistical issues of properly staffing it with so few people. The honest sense was that the task was too great, but that surely the Lord would help them with it, somehow.

As the Talbots were leaving to return home, Shao pulled Daniel aside and said, "P'erry seems somewhat different. Has he secretly begun the conversion process?"

Daniel pondered the matter briefly and said, "In a way, yes. I think it would be fair to say that he is starting to turn toward God. We have seen a lot of improvement in him today."

Shao was pleased. He did not know that the change was largely a result of his *C'lou's* words to P'erry earlier that day.

THE LAST BYE

Chapter III

A Dragon Tail

The very next day was Densed, the tenth day, a day of rest and church. P'erry went, as always, but this time, all of the Corlan could tell that something was different about his attitude. P'erry watched *C'lou* carefully, but she did not render him any special attention. She did not let on in any way that she liked him or that she had spoken to him earlier.

After the meal, while some were dancing in the Spirit and others were getting ready to play fun games, P'erry asked if he could be excused. He told his parents he wanted to be alone. Inwardly, his intent was to find a quiet place to pray.

His parents had told him often how that the Master Himself, the Lord Jesus, had held him at the time of

P'erry's extremely unusual delivery back in the heavenly Jerusalem. Of course, P'erry could not remember that event at all. His parents had also told him how that the Lord had personally visited Sset shortly after their arrival there. P'erry had been far too young then to remember any of that now. Yet P'erry knew the Lord was real, even though he had no memory of ever seeing Him. P'erry was just very uncomfortable with how to relate to God.

He wandered in the direction of the cliffs where he had previously found the Tirra and had wounded the cub. He stopped short of the shore and cliffs. He found a secluded place among the rocks and the undergrowth, and he knelt to pray. The distant sound of the surf crashing against the shore provided a comforting background noise.

He addressed God in simple terms, pouring out his heart in plain honesty. As he confided all of his pain, bitterness, and feelings of being inadequate, salty tears rained on the grassy den. He cried out to the Lord that he wanted to turn his life around and to be changed. He pleaded for God's help. Suddenly an overwhelming power and Presence came into him, expanding his consciousness in indescribable ways. A language that was neither Corlan nor Human erupted from his tongue with an astounding beauty and precision. The sensation of being caught up, of somehow being elsewhere while still kneeling on the ground, amazed him. He lost all track of time. The glory and power of God was upon him so strongly that eventually he lost consciousness.

P'erry had no idea he had been watched there in the little hiding place. A young Tirran had strayed from the pack, and had noticed P'erry's approach. Tirra are not only highly intelligent, but also very perceptive—not only in the natural world, but also in the spirit realm. J'etsu's mother had told him that the evil being that once nearly killed him was filled with darkness. That was literally how she perceived P'erry. When she had looked upon Shao, Daniel, and *Tess*, she saw brilliant light. When she had looked upon P'erry in the cave, she had seen terrible darkness in him.

J'etsu had never before seen either a Corlan or a Human, so he had no frame of reference, nothing to compare to the being he was now watching. Yet he knew darkness when he saw it.

J'etsu thought, *This must be the one who attacked me. The Eldest said there is only one evil being. How could something so small have done so much damage to me? Was I ever that tiny?*

The enormous Tirra stealthily approached, gripped with a terrible fear and ready to leap into flight from all fours at a moment's notice. He watched as P'erry prayed, and before his very eyes the boy was transformed from darkness into brilliant light. J'etsu's fears melted away as he saw the change. Then he watched the tiny figure crumple to the ground. J'etsu came in on all fours and stood over the unconscious form.

It is an understatement to say that the Tirra towered over the boy. The Corlan measure common distances in *ment*. One ment is about six feet, or approximately 1.8 meters. The huge creature stood over two ment at the shoulder (about 12 to 14 feet, almost 4 meters). At the top of his crested head, he was over four ment tall (about 24 to 28 feet, or almost 8 meters).

While standing on the ground, the Tirra seemed to rest on its "feet" regarding the shorter back legs, while resting on its "knuckles" regarding its much taller front legs. Extending upwards from both right and left sets of front knuckles stretched a long, thick, fourth "finger" that was used to extend the wing membrane that was attached to it. (The finger-like wing-tip extensions were of considerable length, almost two ment, or about 11 feet, well over 3.3 meters).

The wings were made of a leathery membrane that stretched from body to legs, connecting each back leg to each front leg, and extending to the entire length of the massive fourth "finger." More of the leathery membrane spanned between the back legs and the long, thick tail.

The Tirra's head was adorned with a tall, plume-like ridge crest, extending down its neck, for channeling wind for steering. As with all males, parts of the crest and face were decorated with a beautiful trim of light purple.

The powerful body, legs and neck were brown colored and about the size and configuration of a Ssettian kelt, which would have been similar to a rather large giraffe back on Earth. Like a giraffe, the Tirra's neck was very long and powerful. Unlike a giraffe, the Tirra's head seemed huge, with a very long, yet lightweight, "beak like" mouth protruding forward.

The Tirra waited and watched. The glow strip in the sky slowly shrank and faded as evening drew on. The massive gas giant, T'and, appeared on the horizon, slowly dominating the night sky, as always.

J'etsu pondered what he might say if and when the tiny being ever regained consciousness. He finally saw a slight stirring as P'erry began to wake, and so he telepathically spoke.

At that moment, while P'erry was still dazed in a mist of glory, and not entirely awake in the natural realm, he suddenly heard a strange voice inside his head.

The voice said, "My mother warned me that you were a being of darkness and evil. Yet I have watched you change from darkness to light. Are you good now? Are you righteous?"

P'erry opened his eyes, blinked, and then rolled over, pushing himself onto his back. A huge, male Tirra was standing over him. At first he thought, *I must be dreaming*. Then a Tirran-sized drop of dragon saliva landed on his forehead. He instantly realized this was no dream. He scrambled backwards, using his elbows to crawl away. The Tirra leaned its massive head sideways to the left, with an inquisitive expression in its eyes.

The voice in his head said, "You *are* good now, aren't you? You *are* righteous. I can tell."

"I am not dreaming. This is real," P'erry said aloud.

The voice in his head said, "You are not dreaming. This is real."

P'erry said, "How are you talking without moving your mouth? How am I hearing you in my head?"

The Tirran explained, "How else would we talk? You have hands. I have wings. You have lips. I have cresps. I cannot form your kind of words with my mouth."

"You speak Corlan?" P'erry stammered.

"Well enough. We learn this language in school. It is a funny language. I like it."

P'erry laughed out loud. The huge creature snorted in a loud way that was both amusing and somewhat alarming. It was apparently how a Tirra laughs.

P'erry asked, "Did the members of the Corlan delegation tell you how sorry I am that I wounded you?"

"They told my mother. I was unable to attend."

"Please forgive me."

"I forgive you."

"Thank you."

After a pause, the creature conveyed, "You are small."

"You are *large!*" P'erry replied, and he laughed again.

After another short pause, the creature then said, "Will you be my issesedondi?"

Issesedondi is the Corlan word for friend. P'erry's heart was pierced with emotion. It was the first time anyone on Sset had asked him those words. Tears came to his eyes.

"Yes. Let's be friends," he answered.

"I have to get back now," the Tirra said. "What is your name?"

"P'erry."

"I like your name. It is funny. My name is J'etsu."

"I know. I remember. I will never forget your name."

"Can you come back here tomorrow?"

"I will try," P'erry pledged.

"Good," the creature said.

With that, J'etsu turned and leaped into the air from all four legs. It extended its immense wings, flapped a couple of times, and then glided away toward the dimly lit shoreline.

In flight, its long neck gave balance and aided with steering. With its long "fourth finger" appendages fully extended, its wingspan was between seven to eight ment or more in width (somewhere between 40 to 50 feet, or almost 14 meters).

P'erry wiped the gooey saliva away from his forehead and ran toward home.

◆◆◆◆◆◆◆

The gathering was sure to be over by the time he arrived. He exuberantly burst through the door of his home.

"Mom! Dad! I am now filled with the Spirit of God! I spoke in another language! I met the young Tirra! We became friends! I love you! I love everybody! We have to go tell them!"

There was no answer. The house was empty. He tore out of the house and ran all the way to Shao's house.

His mother met him at the door, and said, "Uncle Shao doesn't feel well. He collapsed some time after dinner. With all the contaminated food they've eaten for all these denicam, the adult Corlan are beginning to age. He is in there with your father."

P'erry grabbed his mother by the hand, and pulled her behind him. He led her into the room where his father was standing over the Corlan leader.

With a much more calm tone of voice than before, P'erry repeated his good news, "Uncle Shao, Mom, Dad, I am now filled with the Spirit of God. It happened tonight. I spoke in another language. I also met the young Tirra that I wounded. He's very healthy. We became friends. I love you all. Please forgive me for being so rude and mean for my whole life."

Aunt Shao had come in, and she heard the news. She and *Tess* both burst into tears, and they stood hugging each other. Shao motioned for some assistance, and he pulled himself up from the couch. He wept as he hugged P'erry and then Daniel.

P'erry said, "Dad, I want to do the water-covering ceremony, the baptism. Can we get everyone together and do it now?"

"Yes, we can!" Daniel replied.

Daniel had baptized many people in Jesus name during his earthly ministry as a pastor, and each time had given him a thrill. All of those instances paled in comparison to this. Tap, Swov, and Karq had helped Shao to the water's edge.

Shao called out, "We never realized this retention pond would be used for this!"

Daniel explained to all of the Corlan, "Back on Earth, in our mother tongue, the name *Jesus* means Yahweh-Salvation, or in other words, 'the LORD God is become my Salvation, or Savior.' Truly the Lord has become P'erry's salvation.

"Back on our world, Humans were sinful, and we all desperately needed a Savior. The Lord God made Himself known to Humankind in, and as, a perfect Human. He came bearing this wonderful name.

"That perfect, sinless Human, Jesus, was put to death on the Earth to pay the sin-penalty for all who would trust in Him. His dead body was buried under the ground, and then He was resurrected after three days and nights.

"This water symbolizes that ground. P'erry going under the water, and then coming up out of the water, represents him being buried with our Lord under the ground and then being raised with Him from the dead!"

Just then, before the baptism, Shao motioned for everyone's attention.

With a solemn sense of marking the occasion, Shao decreed, "P'erry, from henceforth, you are now Corlan. Even as I received no memories from the surati, it is not a requirement that you receive any memories. To be Corlan requires only pureness of heart. We declare that P'erry is hereby adopted into our family. He is one of us."

Daniel baptized his son in Jesus name.

Suddenly, *Aunt Shao* stepped into the water.

She boldly announced, "Just as P'erry is becoming Corlan, I want to do this righteous Human thing out of respect for our Lord of all cyntu. Please baptize me too."

Daniel baptized her in Jesus name. Then Shao and *C'lou* also stepped in and were baptized. All the Corlan followed them, one by one. The last two were Karq and his son, T'anah.

From the water, Shao shouted, "We are not two peoples. We are one!" Cheers erupted, and many wept.

P'erry hugged T'anah and said, "I'm so sorry for all the wrong I've done to you. Please forgive me."

"Think nothing of it," T'anah said, "I didn't make things easy for you. For that, I am to blame."

C'lou whispered to her mother, "This is the best Densed since the dawn of time."

THE LAST BYE

CHAPTER IV

Flying the Jet

The next day, P'erry talked his parents into coming back with him to meet J'etsu. That took some convincing, because work on the new ship had begun in earnest. HMS Shao II was to be almost twice as large as the first. As each of the Corlan adults had begun to display more gray hair and worse signs of aging, time was becoming a very scarce commodity.

When P'erry's new friend showed up, he also was not alone. P'erry guessed that J'etsu's parents were among the formation of five Tirra that approached them from above. His mind flashed back to the furious mama approaching him on the ledge, wanting to attack him. Naturally, he became worried and somewhat afraid.

As the Tirra group dropped down before them, J'etsu

landed in front. He walked on all fours toward P'erry, and leaned his massive head down near P'erry's face. J'etsu emitted a gleeful chortling sound that was half roar, half purr.

The female Tirra behind J'etsu leaned forward. As P'erry concentrated on her face, he realized it was definitely the mama.

Inside P'erry's head, she said, "A Tirra can only target one person at a time telepathically, so the others cannot hear me right now. You may convey our conversation to them. Say aloud to your people, 'I am in communication with *Jhatsu*.'"

P'erry nodded agreement, and then, in as regal a tone as he could muster, he said, "I am in communication with *Jhatsu*."

Jhatsu's mouth/beak thing emitted a strong chortling sound to let everyone know which Tirra she was.

Her voice in his head then continued, "Say, 'Allow me to introduce Torreq and *Torreq*, the Tirran Eldest. They are the leaders of all the Tirra.'"

P'erry dutifully repeated the statement. A male and female pair standing to the far right of *Jhatsu* nodded downward with their heads, and also emitted strong chortling sounds.

Jhatsu continued, "Say, 'Allow me to introduce Jhatsu and *Jhatsu*. They are the parents of J'etsu, who stands before you.'"

Again, P'erry dutifully repeated the statement, and then *Jhatsu's* husband identified himself.

The females' ridge crests were not as tall as the males, and they had maroon colored trim instead of purple. The adult males were all about half a ment larger than the females as well. Even though J'etsu was already huge, he had some more growing to do before he would become as large as the adults.

Jhatsu made a mild chortling noise that was somewhat different than before. P'erry did not realize that it was the Tirran version of a Human saying "ahem" to discretely indicate that something is being overlooked.

So J'etsu then spoke inside P'erry's head, "My mother is hinting for you to introduce to us the ones who are with you."

"Oh," Perry stammered, "Please forgive me." While turning halfway toward his parents, he addressed the Tirran assembly, "Allow me to also introduce my father, Daniel, and my mother, *Tess*. We are all Corlan now, but we used to be only Human, from a world called Earth, in an entirely different cyntu from this one."

Torreq, the male Tirran Eldest, leaned in and spoke inside P'erry's mind, "J'etsu's parents and our Elders could scarcely believe the report he brought to us. We had not dared to hope that such a transformation could take place. So we have come to see for ourselves. His report is true. You have been changed from darkness to light. J'etsu

49

has indicated that you are now forgiven for your previous attack. We will now permit you to have contact with us."

"Thank you, sir," P'erry replied.

P'erry turned to explain to his parents what had just been said, but the Eldest stopped him by saying, "No need. We will speak directly to your parents now. You and J'etsu may go and play together."

"Thank you, sir!" P'erry said.

As he turned to his new friend, J'etsu snorted in a huge, loud laugh.

"What's so funny?" P'erry asked.

Inside P'erry's mind, J'etsu explained, "Torreq just told me that the 'puny one' and I are free to go and play. He called you 'puny one.' It is funny. He never says 'puny.'"

"I get it," P'erry said dryly. "I get it."

J'etsu snorted again in an even louder laugh.

"What is it now?" P'erry asked.

J'etsu said, "My mother just told me to be careful not to step on you, for you are tiny like a leaf, and I might squish you under my foot. She called you 'tiny like a leaf.' It is funny. She has never said 'tiny like a leaf.'"

"Wow," P'erry said. "I must really look funny to you all." As soon as they got out of earshot of the others, P'erry popped the big question, "Do you think that I could ever ride on your back while you are flying?"

"What if you fell off?" J'etsu asked.

"Hmm," P'erry said, "I suppose we would need some

kind of apparatus to bind us together so that won't happen."

J'etsu said, "If that apparatus is ever made, then I would love to fly with you. I love the word *apparatus*. It is so funny! I have not heard that word used in a long while, but I have always liked it. Until we are united with some kind of *apparatus*, let me pick you up so you can pretend you are flying."

"Alright! And by the way, I love the word pretend. I have not heard that word in a while." P'erry said.

J'etsu leaned down and let P'erry straddle his long, beak-like snout. Once P'erry got in position and steadied himself, J'etsu lifted him to the full height that his colossal neck could afford.

"Woooooooooooo-Hoooooooooooo!" P'erry yelled.

J'etsu began to move his head around, carefully yet quickly. He 'zoomed' P'erry from side to side, from front to back, and even a few dipping, swooping, and climbing motions.

"Oh, my goodness!" P'erry's mom said, as she caught sight of the activity.

"Looks like fun!" his dad said.

"It looks dangerous!" she said.

"Maybe," he said, "but I don't think J'etsu will drop him. Let the kid have some fun."

Later on, P'erry asked J'etsu, "So, how many homes do you have in your migration path?"

"Four," came the answer inside his head. "One here on the mainland and three on islands. The farthest island is our nesting ground."

"Nesting ground?"

"It's where we go for C'alimnet. It's where our cubs are born."

"Ah."

J'etsu leaned in and projected, "So, you are really not from the Corlan nesting ground?"

"No. I could only wish!"

"Where is your nesting ground?" J'etsu asked.

P'erry laughed. Then he sighed. Then he got very quiet. He was thinking about how complicated it would be to explain it all.

"Where are your cubs born?" J'etsu asked again.

Finally, P'erry said, "My parents are from a place called Earth, but I was not born there. I was born in a place called the Heavenly Jerusalem, or just Heaven for short."

J'etsu asked, "How far are those places from the Corlan nesting ground?"

P'erry answered, "Earth is a planet in a cyntu that is completely separate from this one. In this cyntu, there is not any direction you could go from here and ever get there, no matter how far you traveled. Heaven is.... Well, it is not even in a cyntu, I guess. It's its own special kind of place."

"Do you miss those places? Are you going back?"

"I was never on Earth, and I was only in Heaven for a short time. We left there right after I was born. I don't remember it at all. I cannot go to either place now, because I have sinned. The only way for a person who has sinned to get there is to die and then get a new body from God."

"You can do that?!" J'etsu conveyed.

"Yep. My mom and dad already have new bodies."

"So, your mom and dad already died?"

"Umm. No. It's—" P'erry stammered. "They're sort of an exception to the rule. Some of the sin-cursed Humans got their new, immortal bodies without dying first, but in most cases that was only if they were still alive at the end of a certain age on Earth."

"So, what if *you* are still alive at the end of an age here on Sset?" J'etsu asked. "Would you not be allowed to get a new body without dying first?"

"I don't know."

"So, you're not allowed on Earth now, yet sinful people used to be allowed there?"

"Right. My mom and dad were born there during the reign of sin on Earth. All the Humans alive back then were mortal because of the sin curse. Now there are only immortals on Earth."

"What is mortal? What is immortal? Are these Earth words?" J'etsu asked.

P'erry thought a bit, and then said, "Yes. Those are

English words from Earth. I used to think mortal meant only that someone *could* die or *could* be killed, but that's not the main meaning. Mortal tends to mean when someone is *certain* to die. It refers to someone who cannot stay alive forever, no matter how carefully they try. Immortal is sort of the opposite, but it also can mean two things. It can mean that someone cannot die and cannot be killed—*or* it can refer to someone who can be killed, yet they *could* live forever, as long as they are not killed."

J'etsu said, "So I am immortal in one sense, because I will live forever as long as I can stay away from heavy, sharp, flying rocks and the evil people who throw them!"

At that, J'etsu snorted a huge, chortling laugh. P'erry nodded and laughed. He was laughing at J'etsu's laughter as much as at J'etsu's joke.

Finally, J'etsu asked, "What is the history of these words? How did they come to be?"

"I don't know," P'erry said.

J'etsu said, "I am not used to hearing words whose history is unknown. It is not our way. However, I am glad to learn their meanings. You were explaining about your parents' nesting ground. Please continue."

P'erry said, "Back then my mom suffered a really bad injury that made her unable to have children."

J'etsu asked, "Did someone throw a rock at her?"

"No, it was much worse than a rock," P'erry said. "My parents said it was a big thing called 'car.' Anyhow, my dad and mom both served the Lord, even though most of the people on Earth did not. Well, my parents just happened to live until the end of that age. Then the Lord changed them both into immortals—along with many others that served Him faithfully. Most of them had already died, but some of them were still alive.

"After that there was a long time of transition. During that age, mortals and immortals lived on the Earth at the same time. The transition period lasted for 1,000 Earth years, which would be about 103 cam here on Sset. They called it the Millennial Kingdom Age. After that, the time of Human sinfulness was over—except for me. Now only immortals are allowed on Earth."

J'etsu thought for a bit, and then said, "So right now, Sset has one mortal, two immortals who cannot be killed, and a bunch of immortals who can be killed."

P'erry nodded and said, "Yep. That about sums it up."

J'etsu asked, "How did things change from your mom not being able to have children to you being born?"

"Right," P'erry said. "Well, at the end of the Millennial Kingdom Age on Earth, the Corlan Golden Age was ending here, because of the wicked Ettosedondi who refused to share the memories with his infant son. When the baby boy died, his intended surati, which were coming from both the father and the mother, could not find a living child to receive them and the Corlan memories they carried. So the surati expanded their search. They multiplied like crazy and spread across the land, devouring the plant life and even some soil too. They were eating so that they could continue to multiply, trying to find a baby who could receive the memories.

"So, the Lord Jesus allowed my mom to go back in time on Earth to visit her former self and an earlier version of my dad, to get the ova and sperm that were needed to make me. Then the Lord 'made' me in Heaven. I was born there, and then finally I was brought here to be the infant that could receive the memories and stop the Surati Plague."

J'etsu tried to process all this and finally said, "Wow."

"I know," P'erry said.

J'etsu said, "So even though you were made by the Lord in Heaven, you are still sin-cursed—because you came from your parents in the past."

"You got it," P'erry said.

J'etsu said, "Just wait until I tell my parents that my new issesedondi is the hero that saved the Corlan!"

"It was nothing really," P'erry deferred. "I was so small then that I don't even remember it. What's worse, although I have the surati inside of me, I still don't get any of the Corlan memories like the other kids. I guess my body is not exactly Corlan, even though my heart is."

Meanwhile, P'erry's parents were talking to the Tirran delegation about the Corlan dilemma. The Tirra already knew about how the adult Corlan were aging and suffering sickness and about the resulting time crunch in getting the new ship built. The question was what to do.

"How can the Tirra help?" Torreq asked.

Daniel talked about the shipbuilding process. It was then agreed that the Tirra could assist with the transport of tree logs to the construction site. Daniel and *Tess* hoped the added help would mean that the new ship could be built soon enough to save all the Corlan. They were concerned that even with the added help, it might not get built in time.

Finally, it was time for everyone to go home. *Tess* called out for P'erry, and *Jhatsu* summoned J'etsu.

J'etsu said, "Let's visit each other as often as we can!"

"Agreed!" P'erry said.

Perry smiled just about all the way home. His parents were very pleased, but they wondered why he kept muttering the word *apparatus*.

For each of the next few days a batch of gigantic Tirra showed up to help with the shipbuilding project. Their aid was deeply appreciated. Shao carefully explained the particular size of tree they needed to target in their effort.

The Surati Plague had pretty much wiped out all the trees on the Corlan home continent. They had reseeded as soon as possible, across as large an area as they could get to. However, the new trees had not had enough time to grow nearly as tall or as thick as the trees that existed before the plague. This meant that many more trees were needed, and they had to be brought from a larger distance away from the construction site.

The men watched with relief and gratitude as the Tirra continuously arrived with trees that they had ripped up by the roots, which they carried through the air using the claws of their back feet. The creatures were so gigantic and powerful that the trees were not that hard for them to carry.

"They certainly seem motivated to work quickly," Daniel observed.

Shao explained, "The reason why the Tirra migrate is because they don't want to over-harvest the *metsi*, a certain variety of floating ocean plants that they eat for food. When the supply in one area needs time to rebound, they move on. The time is nearing for them to leave. We won't have them available to help for very much longer."

Daniel frowned a bit and said, "Aww, my son will be disappointed to learn that his time with J'etsu is short. It's probably best to warn him anyway so they can enjoy the few days they have left."

P'erry wanted to *fly*. As soon as his Dad told him that there were only a few more days left until the Tirra would need to migrate away, P'erry became even more anxious to find something for use as an *apparatus*. He was not thinking in terms of a saddle. He simply needed a way to hang on.

Somewhere deep inside him, P'erry suspected that if he told his parents about his dream to fly on J'etsu's back, his mom would try to veto it. So, rather unwisely, he did not tell them. If our dear reader has ever done something wrong *after* already having been born of the water and of the Spirit into the Kingdom of God, then the reader will know that the conversion process of redemption does not turn one into a robot who has no freedom to choose, and it does not instantly make one all-wise and unable to sin. Even though one's spirit is regenerated, something of the sin curse lives on in the flesh until the final change unto the glorified, immortal body.

P'erry was wrong to conceal his "flight plan" from his parents, but he was not consciously aware of it. Our capacity to know something yet without consciously knowing it has been the root of many problems. Can any of us truly know his own heart? "The heart is deceitful above all things, and desperately wicked: who can know it?" (Jeremiah 17:9).

As P'erry set out to create an apparatus for flying, he faced a dilemma. There was nothing available to him in the categories of leather, rope, or cloth.

There was no such thing as harvested leather on Sset. No animals had ever died prior to the Surati Plague, so there was no animal skin in use then. During the Surati Plague, even the deaths of many thousands of animals did not yield any usable leather, because the surati ate the dead—fur, leather, bone and all—in its need to multiply.

The Corlan painstakingly made rope by hand, but all the existing rope in the Corlan community was ear-marked for use on the HMS Shao II. Also, all cloth that could be spared was being used to make sails for the ship.

P'erry found himself eyeing his surroundings with a new set of eyes. Apparatus eyes. He was ever mindful of how he might reuse or repurpose something as a way to hang onto his Tirran friend. After thorough searches at home and at school, and carefully perusing the community, he realized with sadness that nothing usable was available. He knew better than to steal, and he was unwilling to even consider it, now that he was filled with the Spirit and living for the Lord. Finally, he decided to borrow.

One day after school, P'erry approached Shao at the shipyard. He was so nervous that he wondered if his voice would even function. He was worried about the conversation needed to accomplish the borrowing. What if Shao asked P'erry what the rope was for? He could not lie. He did his best to hide his nervousness.

"Uncle Shao, sir," he asked calmly, "may I borrow some pieces of rope? I will bring them back soon, and unbro-ken."

"Certainly," Shao replied. He thought nothing strange of the request, and he trusted P'erry.

P'erry thought he was in the clear. He started to walk away. But just then....

"P'erry!" Shao called to the boy.

Uh oh, P'erry thought. *Is he going to ask me what the rope is for?*

"Yes, sir?" he said as he turned back.

"How much time are you getting to spend with J'etsu?" Shao asked with curiosity.

Oh, no! P'erry thought. *I am found out!*

"Well," P'erry answered nervously, "my parents let me go out there once every two or three evenings."

Shao picked up on the boy's nervousness, and said, "It's alright, P'erry. You're not in trouble. I'm just curious to know if you've been able to speak to J'etsu without using your mouth."

"What?!" P'erry said with amazement.

Shao explained, "I understand that you've met Torreq. He is my counterpart among the Tirra. Long ago, when our world was young, Torreq and I became very good friends. As our two peoples multiplied, our duties made it difficult for us to see each other very often. However, we speak to one another fairly often, even when Torreq is far away due to migration. In fact, that was how your father and I knew just where to find you, on the day you ran away. Torreq had seen you, and he had alerted me to your presence there. He thought it odd that a boy should be scaling a cliff wall by himself.

"At first, in the early days of our friendship, Torreq could only hear me if I spoke aloud. However, after we had been talking to one another for some time, one day he heard me think a thought that was intended for him. No other Corlan has ever spent so much time with a Tirra as I did, and none has ever gained this ability. I don't know whether or not it is something only I can do. Even if other Corlan could learn this skill, there remains the question of whether a Human-Corlan could."

P'erry was awed by what he had heard. For a while he said nothing. Finally, he remembered the rope, his reason for being there.

"No, sir," he said. "I have not spoken to J'etsu using my mind, but I will try."

Shao smiled and said, "Good. Let me know how it turns out."

P'erry gathered a supply of rope from the shipyard, and then he made his way home. For the rest of the day, he tried to think thoughts intended for J'etsu. No reply ever came.

I guess it's not working, he thought.

Tess was deeply involved in a desperate research effort to extend the aging, Corlan adults' lives as much as possible. Through using a small amount of the precious seed that was reserved for the New Land, she discovered that one particular plant, named *lithune* (pronounced LIH-thoo-nay) was able to extend their lives until its fruit became contaminated by the genetic alteration. She began to work on purifying a small amount of soil for a greenhouse, so she could harvest some. As she was preoccupied with her work, she did not notice that P'erry had brought home some rope.

"Mom," P'erry asked, "can I go and spend some time with J'etsu?"

"Yes, honey," came a somewhat distracted reply. "Just be back by nightfall."

"Yes, ma'am. I will be," he promised.

He thought to himself, *Yes! It's flying time!*

When P'erry approached the shore near the cliffs, the Tirra were all out flying above the ocean. From across the bay, P'erry scanned the airborne community for J'etsu. There were so many other young males the same age as J'etsu. From a distance, P'erry could not tell one from another. Finally, one of the Tirra broke from the pack and curled its flight path in P'erry's direction. It was J'etsu.

As J'etsu came near, his voice said inside P'erry's mind, "Hey! It's good to see you!"

Without using his mouth, P'erry tried to reply to J'etsu by thinking, *It's great to see you, too!*

No reply came.

Finally, P'erry asked aloud, "Did you hear me thinking, 'It's great to see you, too!' I tried to talk to you with my thoughts, like how you talk to me."

J'etsu made a gurgling sound of curiosity, and then he said inside P'erry's mind, "No, I did not hear you, but keep trying every now and then. I will let you know if I do ever hear you."

"Alright. Look what I brought!" P'erry said, proudly displaying the rope he had borrowed.

"Is this the *apparatus?*" J'etsu excitedly asked.

"You got it!"

"How does it work?"

"Well," P'erry said, "I will tie some ropes around you right here—above your wing arms—and then I will hold onto those ropes while we are flying. I can also wrap some ropes around myself securely, and then tie onto your ropes to connect myself to you. That way, even if lose my grip and fall off, I will not fall to the ground."

"Great plan!" J'etsu commented. Then he asked, "But… the ropes will not choke me, will they?"

"I don't think so. If they do, you just let me know."

"Right."

P'erry attached some ropes to himself, both around the waist, between the legs, and over both shoulders. He essentially tied himself into a five-point harness. Then he tied some ropes around J'etsu's lower neck/upper torso.

Nothing could be fastened around J'etsu any lower than that because his wings spanned all the area between his legs on either side—the wings were attached to the sides of his body all the way between his legs. P'erry then used more ropes to connect his harness to J'etsu's harness.

"Ready!" P'erry said.

"Ready!" J'etsu answered.

J'etsu lowered his neck and his body all the way to the ground, and he allowed P'erry to climb on. Then he slowly stood up, as P'erry got into position.

"Set!" P'erry said.

"Shall I rise now?" J'etsu answered.

"YES!" P'erry shouted with glee.

J'etsu crouched down, and suddenly leaped into the air, powered by the enormous strength in his four muscular legs. At the zenith of his jump, he extended his majestic, expansive wings, and began to flap. He had to push a bit harder than normal, but the difference was barely noticeable.

Even as P'erry was on a flight without asking his parents' permission, so also J'etsu was giving his friend a ride without asking permission. J'etsu was rather leery of anyone from his own people seeing them and realizing what they were doing. So he flew them not toward the ocean, where the Tirra were, but inland toward the mountains.

P'erry's heart raced. Flying was totally exhilarating. It was everything he had hoped it would be. In fact, it was more than he had hoped for or had even imagined. For several glorious minutes, they flew past mountains, valleys, cliffs, and plateaus. In J'etsu's mind, he had mapped out a circuitous route that would take them up the mountain range, then along the river, and finally across the plains back to the coast. While they were flying above the plains on the last leg of the journey, P'erry began to wonder about how high they could fly.

"How high can you go?" P'erry shouted, but the noise of the wind against their faces drowned out the sound of his voice. It seemed that J'etsu had not heard him.

P'erry then silently screamed the same thought toward J'etsu, using only his mind.

"I heard you!" J'etsu answered. "I can fly very high!"

The two were ecstatic, not only because they were flying together, but because P'erry had been able to project a thought into J'etsu's mind. As J'etsu began to climb very, very high to impress P'erry with the altitude he could attain, P'erry's heart was in his throat. Much like when a child on Earth is being given a motorcycle ride and the front rider unwisely accelerates so quickly that the child cannot hold on, so it was with these two. P'erry was in a panic as he began to lose his grip.

Neither of the two knew or considered that while J'etsu's colossal lung capacity enabled him to dive deep into the ocean and fly high into the air, P'erry's much smaller lung capacity did not. Before P'erry could warn

J'etsu that their swift, upward trajectory was causing him to lose his grip, P'erry lost consciousness due to altitude. For a strange split-second, he seemed to be looking at the sky through a black tunnel, which quickly closed in, choking off all light. As the world went black around him, his hands relaxed their grip, and then both flapped loose. P'erry tumbled backwards, and then he was caught by the rope that attached him and J'etsu together.

The rope dragged P'erry against J'etsu's back, and then P'erry's limp body was rolled out onto J'etsu's left wing, still attached via the rope. The young Tirra quickly realized that something had gone dreadfully wrong, and so he flipped forward into a nosedive and headed to land.

P'erry's body then rolled downward, off the front side of the left wing, and out into the air beside J'etsu's neck, still hanging by the rope. The well-made rope was strong, and it easily held the weight of the boy. However, their problems soon worsened.

The ropes around J'etsu began to slip downward, toward his neck and head. This was because they were tied around a thicker part of him, and now that he was diving, his thinner upper neck was pointed downwards, and it was actually beneath the thicker part of his neck, at the shoulders. As the ropes around J'etsu slipped down, P'erry was lowered, and soon his body began to beat against J'etsu's face and eyes. This caused J'etsu to panic, and he began to swing his head back and forth, trying to avoid having P'erry hit against his eyes.

In his panic, J'etsu did not see that the ground was coming up quickly, and he did not properly prepare for landing. At the last moment, he finally saw how close they were to the ground, and he sought to curve the nosedive upwards.

In that instant they were banking hard, with the ground very close beneath them, and P'erry was dangling below J'etsu. Just as J'etsu finally recovered from the near crash, P'erry's right hand was slammed against a large boulder, and a bone in his arm audibly popped as it broke. The increased oxygen and the searing pain caused him to begin to awaken.

J'etsu finally managed to pulled off a rather strained landing, and he carefully lowered the wounded rider to the ground. P'erry had never felt so much physical hurt in all his life, and he could not move his right hand or lower arm without the pain expanding ten fold. P'erry screamed, and then he whimpered and moaned.

"Help!" he cried out. "Help me!"

"I have called for my mother," J'etsu said. "I don't know what happened up there. Are you alright?"

"No," P'erry moaned, "I am not alright. I need my parents. They will know what to do."

Within seconds, *Jhatsu* arrived. Soon afterward, she telepathically communicated to Torreq that help was needed, and Torreq telepathically relayed the message to

Shao. It would take quite a while for P'erry's parents and the Corlan to journey to where P'erry was.

Jhatsu snapped her jaw shut on the ropes that connected the pair, severing the cords with her bite. The ropes that were tied around them individually were just left in place.

She scolded them both for their recklessness. J'etsu bowed his long neck and hung his head in shame. P'erry was in too much pain to respond, but he tried to nod in an acknowledgement to her.

As they waited, P'erry turned pale and began to go into shock. When the Tirra realized he was becoming chilled, they scooped up leaves and ripped up some grass, which they used to cover him as well as they could.

Eventually, help arrived. Both of P'erry's parents came, accompanied by Uncle Shao, *Aunt Shao*, *C'lou*, and *Aunt Swov*. While Daniel began to gather sticks large enough to use for a splint, *Aunt Shao* gave P'erry a drink of some juice from a *tensch* plant. The bitter-tasting herb had a strong anesthetic effect. As she administered the foul-smelling numbing agent, *Tess* administered a scolding. After a pause, *Tess* looked up at *Jhatsu* and thanked her.

As the anesthesia began to mask the pain, P'erry sighed with relief. His Dad returned with some wood that could be made into a splint. He set the bone as well as he could and wrapped the arm tightly in the makeshift splint. Naturally he used some of the rope as well, both for tying the splint and for use as a sling.

Daniel winked at his son as he said, "P'erry, you are *grounded* for a while."

"Yes, sir," P'erry replied. "I don't know if I will ever want to do any more flying."

Secretly, he projected a thought to his friend, "Well, it was really fun, and at least we got to fly once."

"I'm so sorry," came the reply in his mind from J'etsu. "I never meant for you to be hurt."

"I know," P'erry sent back. "Don't worry. My parents are here now. Everything will be fine."

Eventually the Tirra all went back to the shoreline and the non-winged people all went back home.

Shao inwardly admired P'erry for having flown on the back of a Tirra. However, he kept his admiration secret, for the most part, because P'erry had not gotten permission and had gotten hurt. Shao did discuss it with his wife and *C'lou*. His esteem for P'erry caused both of them to esteem P'erry as well. Sadly, not all the Corlan were so inclined.

CHAPTER V

Key Discovery

P'erry slept in. When he finally woke, he was in a considerable amount of pain, both in his arm and in his head. His mother brought him a cup with a tiny amount of *tensch* juice.

She said, "You can take a little bit more of this today, and a tiny bit tomorrow, but we are going to be careful, because *Aunt Shao* told me this stuff is addictive."

P'erry drank the small amount and then said, "Yuck! It smells awful and tastes even worse! How could anyone ever become addicted to *tensch* juice?"

"Honey, you would be amazed if you saw what happened back on Earth. Quite a few people deliberately abused themselves with substances that they consciously knew would kill them, and, once addicted, they never stopped the substance abuse until they actually died."

P'erry had wanted to tell his parents and Uncle Shao about the breakthrough in telepathic communication with J'etsu, but as the anesthetic took hold on him, his mind became too foggy for him to think clearly.

By the third day, P'erry had firmly realized that there were at least two bad side effects of the *tensch* juice. One was that he could not think clearly while he was under the numbing effect. Also, he found that when the effect wore off, it left his head throbbing in a very annoying headache. The overall result was that he tended to become somewhat grouchy.

"Are you hurting badly?" his mother asked.

"Yes, ma'am," he replied, "but I don't want anymore *tensch* juice. I'd rather just take the pain."

"Good boy," she told him.

P'erry finally felt like he was up for moving around and even getting out of the house.

"Mom, can we go to the shipyard today?" he said.

"Why?" she said in a what-in-the-world tone of voice.

"I need to tell something to Uncle Shao, and to you and Dad."

"Alright," she said. "It's nearing lunchtime. You can come with me. But be *careful* with your arm."

Outside, the day was bright under the glow strip, and wonderfully warm. If it weren't for the throbbing pain in

P'erry's arm, it would have been another beautiful day for enjoying life. They made their way through the little town and down to the shipyard.

The partially completed ship showed bare "ribs" that looked like the skeletal remains of the chest of some gigantic, mysterious beast. Near the ship, placed outdoors, there was a long, wide table with benches. On many days everyone gathered there to eat. Although P'erry did not really understand why, his parents called it a "picnic" table. (It was apparently a term from Earth, as the Corlan never used that word.) There was no established seating arrangement, except that Uncle Shao and *Aunt Shao* always sat together at the head of the table (he to the right and his wife to the left).

That day, when everyone took a break to eat lunch, a decent amount of attention was paid to P'erry. He tried to smile through his pain. *Tess* was careful to place their family beside Uncle Shao, just so P'erry could speak to him. She sat P'erry at the end of the table, between Uncle Shao and Daniel. She sat on Daniel's right side. *C'lou* sat on the opposite side of the table, at her mother's left side.

P'erry smiled at *C'lou* and said, "Hello."

She smiled back and said, "Hello. We've been praying for you. It's good to see you up and about."

P'erry had wanted to tell Uncle Shao about the matter privately, but that was not really an option, so he simply spoke rather quietly. The rest of the Corlan around the long table were all talking among themselves, so he felt that he could speak without the others paying much attention.

"Uncle Shao," he said with a muted excitement, "it happened just like you said. I was able to speak to J'etsu without using my mouth!"

Uncle Shao matched P'erry's reduced volume when he answered, "Excellent! I'm thrilled for you, P'erry. If your friendship with J'etsu becomes even half of what my friendship with Torreq is, then you will be a blessed man, indeed. Next to my wife, Torreq is my best friend."

Aunt Shao heard, and she smiled. Daniel had heard them too, and *Tess* had barely been able to hear, only because she was straining to know what P'erry had hinted about at the house, of needing to say something to the three of them. P'erry's parents both spoke at once. Because P'erry and Shao seemed to be almost whispering, they also used hushed tones.

"Excuse me?" Tess asked quietly, shaking her head in wonder.

"Whoa!" Daniel whispered. "Did I just hear what I thought I just heard?"

P'erry looked up at them, and he nodded.

Still speaking quietly, Shao told them, "I told P'erry about my ability to speak to my friend, Torreq, via the unseen realm, without using my mouth. I encouraged him to try this with J'etsu. Apparently, they succeeded. As far as I know, this is the only other instance of it in all the history of our world."

All four of the grown-ups congratulated P'erry and smiled at him. *C'lou* had caught bits of the conversation, and she was able to piece together most of what was said. She truly liked P'erry, and it thrilled her for him to find acceptance and even some honor among her people.

However, Uncle Karq was also watching them from the far end of the table, and although he could not hear what was being said, the expressions he saw on their faces did not go unnoticed. When he finally saw P'erry receive pats of assurance and congratulations, it all frustrated him greatly.

Karq suddenly announced loudly, "Sire, let us congratulate the youth who are helping us so much with the work on the ship! Your grandson, T'anah, has truly mastered some of the woodworking techniques that we have need of!"

"Indeed," Shao replied with a smile, but a slight glint in his eye revealed that he knew something in it was amiss. Somewhat about Karq's demeanor was off, and it did not sit well with Shao.

Several patted T'anah on the back, and applause of appreciation was given for all the youth. Of course, P'erry felt excluded from that appreciation, because his flight stunt and broken arm meant that he was temporarily unable to help with the shipbuilding project.

It was not Karq's explicit intention to make P'erry feel excluded. However, Karq was a bit annoyed by watching P'erry be seated next to Shao and by seeing P'erry get special attention from Shao. It all seemed to place P'erry at a higher status than all of Shao's own blood-related grandchildren. Karq sought to correct this by goading Shao into praising his native-born Corlan offspring.

At each weekly Densed, Shao and some of the adult men were doing less dancing in the Spirit and more sitting around and talking. The pains of aging and some strange, new illnesses were taking their toll.

That following Densed, Karq approached Shao and asked, "Sire, may we talk privately?"

"Certainly," Shao said.

When they had moved away from the others, Karq said, "P'erry's exploit with the Tirra indicates that his conversion experience may be insincere. He deliberately concealed his intentions from you in borrowing the rope, and concealed his intentions from his own parents. This is not the Corlan way. What is to be done about this?"

Shao said, "What would you have me to do about it?"

"Sire," Karq answered, "Some of us question the adoption of P'erry into the Corlan family. We question the wisdom of permitting this to move toward a marriage between him and a Corlan daughter. His parents are truly angels in our midst, but P'erry is *reckless*. And while his parents are more like us, P'erry is not. He is certain to die, according to his parents.

"Father, your own memories are clear in our hearts. At the beginning of our world, your visit to Earth revealed that Humans pass their curse to their *children*. If we permit P'erry to wed a Corlan daughter, won't the resulting children be cursed? Won't they be reckless and deceitful like their father? Won't they needlessly suffer death? Won't that Corlan daughter weep? Won't we all weep over the sorrow her children will bring upon our people?

"Eldest, I beseech you, do not let this come to pass. The longer you wait to address it, the harder it will become."

Shao said, "Karq, hear the counsel of your Eldest. It is true that we expect P'erry to die one day, but we know not when that day will come. We have faith that we will make it to the New Land, and perhaps recover ourselves from the white hair and aching sicknesses you and I now share. Apparently, P'erry's body will finally age this way and never recover from it. When? It could be ten cam, or ten thousand, or more. We know not. Are you so cruel as to consign him to life and death without a mate or the joy of children? Without the right to procreate?

"He bears the name of a long-dead Human. It is appointed unto the Humans to suffer death, but because of this, they have a custom to give the name of the dead or dying unto their offspring. In so doing, they preserve the name alive. Are you so cruel as to steal from his fore-father this meager Human right, already bestowed and lawfully exercised?

"You speak of what is not the Corlan way. Yet this cruelty that you propose is not Corlan.

"You point out that P'erry is reckless, yet it was Corlan recklessness that brought upon us the Surati Plague. Consider that there are at least two kinds of recklessness. One rebels against God, doing what God forbids. Another explores what God allows, taking advantage of that which has not been forbidden. Be careful when speaking to me about recklessness!

"I grant that the Corlan lack the *recklessness* to do such mighty deeds as mounting the back of a befriended Tirra and flying above the very atmosphere. I declare to you that what we lack, P'erry may teach us, and what he lacks, we may teach him. I pray we don't teach him so much that he loses what makes him unique and powerful."

A terrible coughing welled up from the deepest parts of Shao's lungs, interrupting him for a time.

Then he continued, albeit more weakly, "All my life I longed to ride the back of Torreq, yet I lacked the recklessness to do it. Now I suffer age and sickness, and I may never be able to fulfill that dream.

"You point out that P'erry is different. Thank God he is. Mark my words: That difference will save our people. He is the key. He will figure out what we are unable to, because he lacks our lack of creativity, our lack of reck-lessness, and our lack of ability to see the obvious."

Karq hung his head in shame during the rebuke. Finally, Shao hugged him and squeezed him.

"I love you, my son," Shao said, "but please do not fear the plan God has put into action. God would not impose ability and drive to procreate while withholding the right to do so. If He meant for P'erry to have a Human wife, then He would have provided one. There is surely a reason why the surviving Corlan youth are an odd number, with an extra female in the waiting. Don't fear to allow God's will to unfold. Who knows where the path may lead? Be reckless enough to walk that path. Trust in God, and trust in my leadership under Him."

"Yes, sire," Karq said demurely.

Thankfully, P'erry was left handed, so the broken right arm did not stop him from writing at school or at home. However, it meant that the shipbuilding work progressed even more slowly because there was one less able-bodied person. As the adult Corlan, especially some of the men, showed more and more signs of aging, P'erry tried to assist as much as he could. He ran errands and carried items with his good hand.

Once each Densed, P'erry was permitted to go and seek out J'etsu, after having pledged to his parents that he would not try any stunts without permission. After a couple of weeks with his arm in the sling, he no longer suffered any pain, but he still wore the splint.

On the thirty-third day with his arm in a sling, he was surprised to see J'etsu in the air over the shipyard. P'erry was excited yet also saddened. He realized that J'etsu was likely coming to say goodbye.

As J'etsu approached, P'erry tried several times to communicate with him from a distance. J'etsu did not respond.

Several people noticed the approaching Tirra, and they paused in their work to watch him land. J'etsu and P'erry met near the "picnic" table.

With profound sadness J'etsu said, "I could have said so from among my people, but I wanted to tell you face to face that we are leaving tomorrow."

P'erry ran to him and buried his face in J'etsu's thick brown fur, which had a salty smell of the ocean clinging to it. P'erry decided that he would never forget that smell.

"I will miss you my *big* friend," P'erry said with his mind, and his tears flowed.

"I will miss you my *puny* friend," J'etsu said. The creature's expressive eyes were forlorn and pitiful.

P'erry thought for a minute, and then projected, "When you arrive at your second home after the migration, talk to me from a distance. If I can hear you, I will respond 'I heard you.' If you can hear me, then you say the same thing!"

"Right. Sounds like a great plan. I have to go now."

"Bye."

"Bye. We will pray for you all."

"Thanks."

With that, J'etsu turned, leapt into the air, and soared away. P'erry looked up and watched until the sight of his friend disappeared in the distance. The he bowed his head and wept. His tears dropped onto the wooden splint.

Uncle Shao approached him to offer comfort, and said, "The face to face part of a friendship is truly wonderful, but the heart to heart portion is the most important, and no separation or distance can take that away from you two."

"Yes, sir," Perry acknowledged.

At that moment, for some reason, P'erry remembered a portion from a Scots poem that his parents had taught him from ancient Earth history. It was the part that says: "The best-laid plans of mice and men often go awry."

Two days later, in the evening, the voice of his friend came into his head, "Hello! It's me! Can you hear me?"

P'erry responded, "I heard you!"

"Excellent!" J'etsu said. It took me a while to find you."

"What do you mean? How did you find me?" P'erry queried.

"In order to talk to you from a distance, we use a kind of movable tunnel or hole. My parents taught me to call it a window when talking to you. While we were on the mainland, I knew just where to move the window. After we made it to the island, I had to relearn where to move the window."

"Wow!" P'erry said, although he did not understand in the least what J'etsu was talking about. "Well, I'm just glad you got it figured out.

The two were excited to be able to communicate from a distance. From then on, they spoke from time to time.

Several times afterward, P'erry tried to initiate communication with J'etsu, but it never worked. He could only talk with his friend whenever J'etsu initiated the conversation.

After about four more weeks, P'erry's arm was again examined and finally deemed completely healed. He was so very thankful to be free from the splint and sling and glad to be able to help with the shipbuilding project.

P'erry's life was now dramatically different, for the better. Each weekday he tolerated school, happily exchanged hellos and smiles with *C'lou*, enjoyed working on the ship, and spoke to J'etsu without seeing him.

Uncle Swov and *Aunt Swov* had approached him to explain that if J'etsu were to contact him during school, he would need to reply that he was in school and that he would have to talk later. P'erry obeyed.

Tolerating school was the only downside. Yet it was in school where P'erry learned something that was crucial in helping the Corlan make it to the New Land.

A Corlan school on Sset is substantially different from a Human school on Earth. Due to the encoded, ancestral memories transferred via the surati, all the Corlan males know all the early memories of their male ancestors (from each ancestor's youth up until the time when the next ancestor in their line was born), and the same is true of Corlan females, except they get the early memories of their female ancestors. This results in various, different "familial" lines of memory spanning back to the beginning of their existence.

While they all share in common the earliest memories of Shao (for males) or *Shao* (for females), no two Corlan families share the rest of their memories in common. Their schooling is an effort toward having all memories in common, so to speak. Each family line seeks to share whatever knowledge, wisdom, or experience it has gained that makes it unique or disparate from the others.

Naturally, such a process would not suit a Human boy who has no memories other than his own. Uncle Swov and *Aunt Swov* had tried to accommodate P'erry. They had done their best to help the boy gain a working knowledge of Corlan history, customs, wisdom, and know-how. P'erry presented a challenge that had caused the Swov's to become innovative. They used what might be called "Human" methods—reading, writing, singing of songs, audio and visual rehearsal/repetition, games, and so on—you name it, they tried it.

During P'erry's early years, the Swov's had faced an uphill battle in trying to get P'erry to commit to memory names, dates, places, and events which had no context for him and for which he simply did not see any need. Now that P'erry was more accepted as a Corlan, he was more interested. Plus, he was a little older and a little more mature. Their lives as teachers were somewhat easier.

Eventually the Swov's realized that the use of object lessons and illustrations helped P'erry to grasp a thing or, at least, helped to catch his interest long enough for them to explain a thing. Over time they became skillful at this.

When *C'horat's* Theory was mentioned in passing one day, those in the room with inherited memories knew and understood the concept. Yet P'erry did not. When he expressed curiosity about it, Uncle Swov thought up a way to explain. He had his wife to cover for him while he left the class. He quickly returned with some very soapy water and a wooden ring attached to a wooden dowel rod. He soaked the "bubble wand" in the sudsy water, and began using it to blow bubbles.

This sight captivated P'erry's attention. He listened intently as Uncle Swov reviewed some of what had already been taught but not in quite the same way. Uncle

Swov explained that each and every body of mass (within their cyntu) is surrounded by a bubble-shaped gravity well, a spherical distortion of space-time. The Corlan name for it is *sedondi*. The sedondi surrounding a person (or any object of relatively little mass) is rather minor and practically imperceptible. However, around planets and stars, the field is observable, in the form of a dome, or partial dome, of rocks, debris, stellar gases and energy, etc., caught in the gravity trap that surrounds the mass.

For example, their star, called P'av, had a massive, very hot sedondi around it. Also T'and, a gas giant that was orbiting their star, had a formidable sedondi. Sset, their home world, was actually a moon orbiting T'and.

Swov kept blowing bubbles as he spoke. Then he gave the bubble wand to his wife, and began to draw an illustration while she continued to blow bubbles.

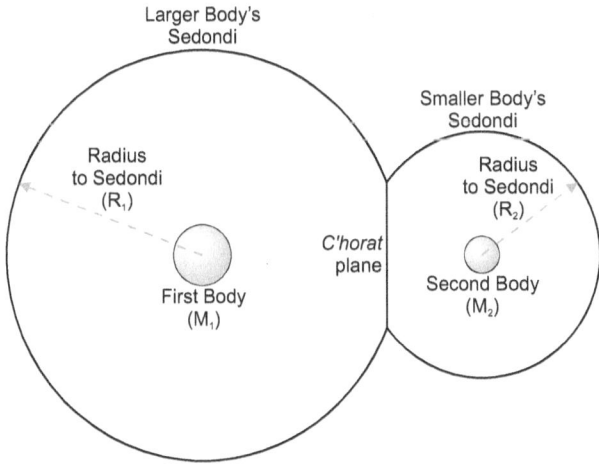

P'erry said, "So where does *C'horat's* Theory come in?"

"Well," Uncle Swov said, "let me remind you that the sedondi of our star intersects with the sedondi of our gas giant. The collision between the two causes the trase-dondi, our glow strip, where the super-heated material in the star's sedondi transfers massive amounts of energy to the relatively cold material in the gas giant's sedondi. It is how God provides us with life-giving light and heat.

"*C'horat's* Theory is about the area created when any two sedondi intersect. *C'horat* was a brilliant Corlan scientist. She died in the Surati Plague. All the adults knew her well. Your mother reminds us of her sometimes. The theory goes something like this:

"Whenever two bodies of equal mass are positioned so that their sedondi intersect, the gravitational distortions from both bodies are equal, and therefore they cancel each other out, meaning that the area where the two sedondi intersect should be free from any space-time distortion.

"Furthermore, even if the two bodies are of *unequal* mass (yet similar enough to be within a certain limit), they will still exert equal amounts of distortion at the plane of intersection, and they will still cancel each other out. This is because the amount of distortion is not only proportionate to the mass of the object, but also inversely proportionate to the distance from the object—and the smaller object will always be *closer* to the plane of intersection than the larger one, and proportionately so.

"Again, both bodies will exert some force of distortion of space-time in the plane of intersection, but the effect of each will be cancelled out, by the equal force of the other body. The very simple equation looks like this."

He wrote out an equation and then explained, "Take the mass of the larger first body (abbreviated M_1) multiplied by the *sedondi constant* (O), which yields the radius (R_1) to its sedondi (the distance from the object's center of gravity to its outlying spherical distortion field). Repeat that for the smaller second body ($R_2=M_2O$). Then, calculate the force (F_1) of distortion applied by the larger first body, which is its mass (M_1) divided by its radius (R_1). Repeat to calculate the force of distortion applied by the smaller second body ($F_2=M_2/R_2$). As you can see, F_1 will always equal F_2."

P'erry was not really getting it, so Uncle Swov went back to using the bubbles to explain. This was what he had planned all along. He used the wand to produce a batch of bubbles, and then he selected a big bubble by touching it with the ring of the wand. It stuck. Then he used the wand to guide the larger bubble over to a smaller bubble. As he touched the two together, they stuck to each other. He then slowly turned the wand so the two bubbles were pointed downward, so that the smaller bubble would not touch the wand.

The two bubbles then had a completely flattened plane of soap film where they mutually shared a "bubble wall."

At the area where they touched, the sides of each of the two bubbles were united, and notably, that area was not curved at all.

Uncle Swov said, "Imagine that the big and small bubbles are the two intersecting sedondi of a large body of mass and a small body of mass. Now, look closely at the area where they touch. That represents the area of intersection, which we now call *C'horat's* plane, or just 'the *C'horat'* for short.

"Do you see how that area of intersection, the *C'horat*, is a flat plane? It is not curved inward on the side of the small bubble, nor is it curved inward on the side of the larger bubble. Admittedly, we know that the soap film achieves its flatness in this area for an entirely different reason—surface tension—than does the space-time between two sedondi—matching gravitational forces—but you get the basic idea: wherever any two sedondi intersect, there is no distortion of space-time. No bending whatsoever."

"Wow!" P'erry exclaimed, "That is something I can actually understand! Did she ever have time to prove or disprove her theory?"

Uncle Swov answered, "She formed the theory long before we had a way to test it. However, prior to the Surati Plague, she was finally using the newly built Telmis Observatory to gather and catalog data. All her preliminary readings supported her theory. Since her death during the plague, no one has had time to continue her research. Based on what I saw, I believe her theory to be true and correct."

After school that day, P'erry wandered over into the desolate heart of the abandoned, ancient Corlan city, or what was left of it, at least. It was clear that this place had contained the pinnacle of Corlan architecture, arts, and sciences. Any and all wooden structures were gone, having been eaten by the surati during the plague, but stone structures and metal items remained intact.

Suddenly he heard a noise behind him. He whirled around to see R'ei, *B'rei*, and *C'lou* following him. He smiled and waved to them.

From a distance, *C'lou* said, "Hey, P'erry, where are you going? We saw you head away from the shipyard, and we got curious. What's up?"

"Nothing much," P'erry said. "I wanted to see if I could find the Telmis Observatory. I'm just exploring a little."

P'erry paused and waited for them to catch up.

"Can we join you?" R'ei said.

"Sure."

B'rei said, "The Telmis Observatory was that way, just beyond the Council Chambers of the Elders."

P'erry smiled and said, "Thanks."

C'lou said, "I have not been here in a long time, but my memories of my ancestors' knowledge of the city are sharp and clear. What a difference between then and now."

R'ei said, "It was a terrible thing what the Ettosedondi did—withholding the memories and letting his infant son die of starvation, wiping out our people."

B'rei commented, "Up until that point, many believed the Lord's prophecy about the Ettosedondi was true, yet they always imagined it to be thousands of cam away, in some far distant future. They never thought it would happen so soon."

They made their way past the Council Chambers and through the few buildings still standing between there and the observatory. The Telmis was as ornate as any other building, and it had a metal roof—still somewhat shiny—that was unique because of its sliding panel opening. The roof had been left open at the time of the plague, and so it had been standing open ever since. The unbelievably large telescope was still peeking out, staring out toward the sky.

"This is amazing!" P'erry said, nodding in awe.

"You got that right," R'ei affirmed. "New memories."

The doors were standing open. The kids walked in. There was some evidence that backslidden Corlan looters and rioters had scavenged the building during the plague.

C'lou pointed to a spiral stairway made of metal and said, "I think this is the way to the observation deck."

The kids excitedly ran to it and climbed to the top floor, which granted access to the main telescope.

A complex series of knobs, crank handles, gears, pulleys, and other technology was there that had originally allowed for practically effortless control of the telescope.

"It's a reflector type," P'erry said.

"A what?" R'ei asked.

"My Dad has taught me a little about the telescopes in Earth's history. There were two main types. At first, the refractor telescopes were used. Then, later, reflector telescopes were invented. This is a reflector type."

"How can you tell?" *C'lou* asked.

P'erry pointed and said, "See that round mirror-like thing with the tarnish showing on the edges? That's the reflector. It's where the observer—called an astronomer back on Earth—would see the magnified image of things floating out in space."

"That is... amazing!" *B'rei* said.

"You got that right," R'ei affirmed. "New memories."

"You keep saying that," *C'lou* said to R'ei.

He just smiled and said, "Well, it's true. After we make it to the New Land, there will be no way to get in and see this, but our offspring will be able to remember seeing it because of our memories. This is an epic adventure."

C'lou and *B'rei* nodded, but at the mention of the memories, P'erry turned and walked away.

C'lou noticed, and she followed him.

"P'erry, what's wrong?" she asked.

P'erry turned, then bowed his eyes and shook his head

slowly. Finally he decided to answer openly.

"I'm still kind of sensitive about the fact that I'm not getting any memories from the surati, even though I've had them since the beginning."

C'lou had enough of her father in her that she knew how to answer him.

"P'erry, of all the Corlan who ever lived, none but you have ever flown on the back of a Tirra. The only one to ever do that is one *without* the memories. Not to mention, the surati you have came from the Ettosedondi. If I were you and I had his memories in me, I would not want the surati to work right. I would not want to remember him and how he sinned. Did you ever stop to think, maybe it's a blessing that you don't remember?"

P'erry smiled and wrinkled his nose as he pondered what she had said. He had never thought of it that way, but it actually made sense.

R'ei said, "Hey, everyone at the shipyard is going to be wondering where we are. We need to get back there."

"Right," said P'erry.

As they turned to leave, P'erry noticed something. The light from the sky cast a shadow of the control cabinet on the sidewall. The top of the shadow had a lump.

"There's something on top of that cabinet," P'erry said. He asked R'ei, "Would you help me up?"

R'ei clasped his hands together, and held P'erry's foot while he stood up and grabbed the top of the cabinet. He reached over, and pulled down a beautiful spyglass.

"What is it?" R'ei asked.

"I think it's a spyglass, a small, handheld telescope," P'erry said.

He pulled on the ends to expand it to full length, bringing its three "telescopic" sections into their fully opened positions, and then he lifted it up and looked through it.

"Wow!" he said, "several powers of magnification. And I expected to see chromatic aberration. There is none."

"What does that mean?" C'lou asked.

"You know how a prism breaks white light apart into stripes of rainbow colors? Back on Earth, in the early days of telescopes, it took people quite a long time to figure out how to make a telescope that did not have a rainbow of colors around the image, distorting the view. The colors were pretty, but they kept you from clearly seeing whatever it was you were trying to see. Whoever made this one really knew what they were doing."

"Can I see?" she asked.

"Sure."

All the kids took turns looking through the spyglass.

Finally, P'erry said, "This could come in very handy during our voyage to the New Land. We should take this back to the shipyard."

"Good thinking," R'ei said.

On the way back to town, C'lou told P'erry, "You are so

smart. You know a lot of interesting and important things."

P'erry raised his eyebrows in shock. He had spent his entire academic career feeling ignorant, slow, and behind the curve, compared to the memory-enhanced Corlan. Now, all in one day, he had actually grasped a complex concept in school and had impressed his friends with "trivial" knowledge from his parents that he had thought would never be needed or helpful.

It was the first time of his life when P'erry actually felt pleased about his own intellect. That meager confidence was the start of something great. Feeling confident is so much more productive than feeling ignorant, inadequate, and slow.

"Thank you," he responded. "I appreciate the kind words. By the way, I think you are a *genius*."

He had spoken the word *genius* in English, not Corlan. His father had used it to compliment his mother, and he wanted to compliment *C'lou*, so he said it to her.

"What is 'genius'? Is that an Earth word?" *C'lou* asked.

"Um, yes. Sorry," P'erry said. "My parents sometimes mix Corlan and English—that's their original language from back on Earth—and sometimes I catch myself doing the same thing. Genius means a really, super smart person. My mom is one. Back on Earth, she was one of the smartest people in all of Human history. Somehow my dad never minded her being smarter than him, and so she never minded it either."

"Do you actually think I'm smarter than you?" she asked.

"Absolutely," he said, without a moment's hesitation.

She shook her head and laughed.

"Well, thank you," she responded. "I appreciate your kind words. However, and by the way, I think *you* are a genius."

P'erry rolled his eyes and shook his head. They both laughed.

Later, whenever the two boys arrived at the shipyard, they stood to be scolded for being late for work, but when they produced the spyglass as a tool for the voyage, their lateness was forgotten. P'erry's dad gave a three-minute history lesson about spyglasses on Earth, and P'erry and R'ei received pats on the back for finding and retrieving such a great tool.

Afterward T'anah said, "It's about time you two made it to work. I was starting to get frustrated over being the only boy here. Where were you two anyway? What were you doing?"

R'ei said, "We went on a little adventure into the old city. You should have come. It was amazing."

"Well," T'anah said, "no one told *me*."

They could tell that T'anah was upset because of feeling left out. P'erry remembered the holy words that his father had taught him: "A gentle answer turns away wrath, but a harsh word stirs up anger" (Proverbs 15:1).

P'erry said, "Sorry about that. We didn't mean to not invite you. I originally intended to go by myself, but then the others saw me leaving and got curious. Next time we'll be sure to tell you too, in case you want to go."

"Thanks," T'anah said. His anger melted away. He felt embarrassed afterward, and said, "I'm sorry about what I said just then."

"No problem," P'erry said.

Chapter VI

Banner Furled

At lunchtime the next day, all the kids from school were just arriving at the shipyard to eat with the adults, when *Tess* approached everyone with a huge smile.

Before she even made it to the table, she shouted, "I have the firstfruits from my lithune garden! This fruit is not contaminated!"

They all ran to her with excitement. The tiny harvest was not enough for everyone, and it was instantly decided that the adults who were suffering the worst detriments of age and sickness should get the meager amount of the fruit.

Tess glowed as she gave sections of the beneficial fruit to Shao, Karq, and Swov. (Somehow Tap was not yet as ill or aged, and he was happy to prefer the others before himself. The ladies were all fairing some better than those three men, as well.)

On their way back to the table, P'erry quietly said to T'anah and R'ei, "Hey, why don't we ask permission for another adventure into the old city after school today? Maybe we can find some other tool or something that might be helpful for the voyage."

"Alright," T'anah said.

"Count me in," R'ei said with a big smile.

C'lou overheard them, and she said, "Hey, don't you think some of the girls might like to go too?"

P'erry was inwardly hoping for a chance to become better friends with the other boys, and he somehow sensed that not only were their chances slimmer for getting approval if the girls also wanted to go, but also the boys all acted somewhat differently whenever the girls were around, almost as if they had emotional shields up, or as if they felt a need to show off in front of the girls. A flicker of apprehension crossed P'erry's face, and *C'lou* saw and noticed it.

T'anah came to the rescue by saying, "This is nothing against you girls, but sometimes we guys want to do 'guy stuff.' Just us. All we ever do lately is school and ship-building work. Come on! Besides, if the girls want to go, they'll probably tell us all no."

C'lou smiled a cute half-smile and begrudgingly said, "Oh, alright. I suppose."

She noticed the look of relief on P'erry's face. Although she longed to go on another adventure with them, it pleased her to see a chance for P'erry to become better friends with the other two boys.

Back at the table, each boy approached his own father to request permission. Each got a tentative if-it's-alright-with-your-mother kind of response. P'erry thought it might help if they got Shao's approval at that point.

"Uncle Shao, sir," he asked, "yesterday we took a brief trip into the old city, and we brought back the spyglass, which should be really helpful on the voyage. We three boys were wondering if we could make another short trip today after school."

Uncle Shao was feeling very benevolent after having eaten a few bites of uncontaminated lithune. He felt a little bit lighter and happier, and he wanted to celebrate.

"That's a great idea," Shao declared. "But perhaps one or two of the men should go with you boys. If I am feeling up to it later—"

Just then, a gut-wrenching spell of coughing hit him. Something came up from his lungs. He grabbed his cup from the table, which had not yet been filled with drink, and he turned his head from the others and spit something into the cup. *Shao* and the daughters, *C'lou* and *Karq*, ran to him. When he turned to face the others, he was pale and wobbly.

He weakly said, "Swov, perhaps it would be better if you went with the boys. It seems it's going to take more than a few bites of uncontaminated lithune to get me back to health."

They got Uncle Shao to his seat at the table, and *Tess* motioned to *Aunt Shao* to be shown what was in the cup. She took one long, hard look, and grimaced in obvious concern.

Daniel looked at her, and silently mouthed an English word, "What?" He knew that the Corlan would not be able to read their lips when using English terms.

She followed suit, mouthing back to him a single English word, "Cancer."

Aunt Shao had no idea what they were saying, but she noticed both the fact that they had shifted into silent mouthing of unknown terms as well as the somber expressions on their faces. She grew somewhat faint, and quickly took her seat beside her husband.

Daniel very tactfully said, "There will be more uncontaminated lithune to come. Right now, let's gather and pray for our Eldest."

They all gathered around Shao, and prayed earnestly for him.

C'lou realized that she was not going to want to go on any adventure that day. She wanted to do nothing except to stay by her father's side.

◆◆◆◆◆◆

Later on, after Swov dismissed school, he went with the three boys into the ancient city. He took them into the large, multi-storied building called the Council Chambers of the Elders, and there he showed them where Shao and the other ancient Elders had met to decide on important matters or to settle any and all significant debates.

In the main chamber there still stood a huge, round, stone table. However, all the wooden chairs were gone, having been devoured by the rampant surati. The table's smooth, shiny top was chiseled out of a shale-like stone. Legs of cut limestone supported it. An undisturbed layer of dry, powdery, inert surati covered the tabletop, rendering it a light purple color. More of the lavender stuff covered the floor as well.

P'erry observed, "The tabletop is far bigger than the doors. How did they get this table in here?"

Swov smiled and said, "This table was installed before the walls went up. In the same way that families are built around marriages, and communities are built around families, this structure was built around this table, which was carefully fashioned for the sole purpose of serving wise counsel."

Swov walked over to the table, dusted the powdered surati away from an area at the edge, and laid his hands on the cool surface. He guided the boys to do the same.

He told them, "All of the Elders who ruled here are

now dead, except for Shao and Tap." As he called out the two names he pointed to where their chairs had once been located.

He took three steps to his left, and stopped.

He said, "Shao once told me that this very spot is where Straf stood and challenged all the Elders, demanding that he and other younger men be allowed to rule the Corlan people.

"Someday in the future, some child may question, thinking that if only the Elders had handed the rule of the people over to the rebellious one, then the Surati Plague might not have happened.

"Had Shao and the Elders surrendered, it would have been the downfall of our people, and the plague would still have happened. They stood strong and spoke the truth in love. We must not ever think that appeasement —giving in to rebellion—is an acceptable way to placate the wicked and supposedly prevent catastrophe.

"Also, we must not blame those who stood strong for righteousness, as though they caused the catastrophe. The Elders did not cause the Ettosedondi to do his terrible deed. He chose his own path.

"If we focus only on what was taken away, we may mistakenly think that the wrong option was the better one, or perhaps just that neither option was any better than the other. Such views would be incorrect because they focus only on the loss. We must also consider what remains. Had the Elders yielded to Straf in an attempt to appease his rebellion, nothing would be left today.

"If the Elders had surrendered their rule, they would have been disobeying God. Bear in mind that God had foreseen the wicked choice of the Ettosedondi. At some time Straf was going to do what he did. That's the only point that requires no speculation.

"If the Elders had displeased God by yielding to the rebellion, then Straf would *afterward* have still withheld the memories—perhaps with another child if not with his first—and then God would not have sent P'erry to us. Instead of a remnant surviving, all would be dead.

"Yet because some did what was right, not only during that moment of challenge but also in the times of decision that followed, we are here today. A remnant still lives. A few Corlan remain; ready to repopulate the New Land for the Lord.

"We must always consider what remains, not focus solely on that which was taken away."

Swov then took them to the nearby Aldyn Prayer Tower. The building's outer beauty wowed P'erry, but that did nothing to prepare him for the sacred experience that awaited them inside. Even after all that time of the tower's prayer halls being silent due to the plague, a thick anointing of God's Spirit still abode in the walls and benches, in the very air of the rooms. The dousing was so palpable and holy that the boys nearly fell to their knees when they opened the doors of the first floor's prayer hall. Swov immediately wept as he remembered the many times he had prayed there, of the sweet times of communion with God that he had experienced in the now quiet spaces.

Swov knelt at one of the stone benches and began to pray. The three boys all did likewise. Their voices reverberated through the building's broad chambers. After some time, the boys stood, but Swov prayed on. They stood reverently, with their heads bowed, as their teacher continued in prayer. Finally, he also stood.

He told them, "During the earliest days of the Surati Plague, so many Corlan came here so often to pray, seeking God for strength and guidance to face our darkest hour. At that time, Shao had banners made for each prayer hall, with the same wording on all of them."

He gestured toward the wall behind them, and they turned to see the banner, apparently torn down by backslidden rioters, yet still legible on the floor.

In bold, Corlan lettering it said, "DESPERATE MEN FOR DESPERATE TIMES."

A sharp pang of sacred nostalgia raced through their hearts as they read the words. P'erry suddenly imagined the thousands of faithful Corlan who, knowing they would soon face their deaths, gained from God through prayer the strength to meet their end as noble, righteous people of God instead of backslidden, cannibalistic thugs.

"Sir," P'erry asked, "Why didn't the surati devour this banner? May I gather it up, so that we can take it to the New Land as a memorial of what happened here?"

Swov said, "P'erry, I know don't know how it wasn't devoured. But yes, that would be a good thing to do."

As the other two boys helped P'erry carefully roll the sacred and history-laden sign, P'erry's mind recalled a moment in his childhood there on Sset when his mother had recounted for him a time she remembered from back on Earth. It was the funeral of a professor who was a retired solider—a kind of soldier called a Marine. *Tess* had told P'erry how she had wept as she watched living Marines honor the memory of the fallen, by carefully folding the national flag—a banner of sorts—of their homeland, the United States of America. P'erry thought to himself, *we are doing for the righteous dead Corlan something similar to what those Marines did back on Earth.*

For the rest of that day, a haunting melody that his mother had sung to him echoed through his mind. She had said that the name of the song was "Taps."

Every few days, *Tess* would bring a little bit more of the wonder fruit. Everyone hoped that the tiny amounts of uncontaminated fruit would preserve the lives of the adult Corlan long enough to get the ship built and make it to the New Land.

Tess had to be extremely careful in sowing, fertilizing,

watering, manually pollinating, and harvesting the fruit. Normally the *ginz* (the equivalent of honey bees on Earth), as well as other insects and natural wind, would all take care of pollination. However, inside *Tess'* greenhouse, neither wind nor ginz nor any insect could be tolerated, as it would possibly introduce the altered DNA of the contaminated lithune plants outside.

Because *Tess* lived and worked outside of the greenhouse, she was also a serious risk to it. There was a real danger of carrying pollen in from contaminated plants outside. She had to go through an extremely careful process to check for even the slightest amount of pollen before entering the greenhouse. It was painstakingly difficult, but the payoff was worth it. The greenhouse would never produce enough fruit to mitigate the Corlan need to go to the New Land, but it might just increase how many Corlan lived long enough to make it there.

Shao's and Swov's beards and hair began to see a mixture of black in with the gray, and Karq's hair and beard started to show some blond mixed in. Their aches and pains were reduced. Everyone rejoiced.

Tess' harvesting of the precious lithune fruit went on for several weeks, but then tragedy struck. One day she opened the door to the inner chamber, and heard a buzzing sound. A ginz had made it in somehow. She quickly shooed it out, while wondering how many of her plants might have been affected. She also wondered how the ginz had gotten in.

That day, at lunchtime, she sorrowfully relayed the news that the meager harvests of uncontaminated fruit might well be ending. Indeed, the very next batch of the fruit displayed the lumps and horns that indicated contamination.

Refusing to surrender to discouragement, *Tess* started all over again. Shao permitted her another tiny ration of the uncontaminated seed that was reserved for the New Land, but he advised her that they had reached the limit of how much they could spare. If this second attempt were sabotaged, there would be no more.

Tess went over every inch of the greenhouse in careful examination. She finally found one place where, apparently, some animal had damaged the corner of the greenhouse, probably while it foraged in her regular garden. There a tiny hole was found. That was how the ginz had gained access. She sealed it up, and asked for help from Daniel and P'erry to fortify the greenhouse to prevent such a reoccurrence.

The Last Bye

CHAPTER VII

Mantle

While Daniel and P'erry worked to secure *Tess'* "Greenhouse Version 2.0," she also turned her attention to another avenue of research: Why were Shao, Swov, and Karq aging more quickly than the others? Why were those same three ill more often than anyone else? Tap was not having nearly as hard a time as the other three men. The four adult ladies were also not struggling nearly as much. Why were those three men suffering the worst?

She got all the adults to agree to participate in her study, at least as much participation as they could spare.

"Your very lives may depend on answering my questions honestly," she told them all.

They all pledged to answer her forthrightly. Her first

interview was with Tap.

"What do you do that they don't do?" she asked.

"I don't know," he said. "Nothing that I can think of."

"Alright then," she said. "What do you *not* do that they do? A food, a pastime, a recreation, a place, a habit."

Tap quickly said, "I don't chew *lippet*. They all love them. I hate them now."

"Lippet?" *Tess* inquired.

"They're berry-like buds from the *telumni* bush. The other men chew them as breath fresheners. I can't stand the flavor of them anymore."

Tess then interviewed the sick men's wives. They all echoed the same sentiment as Tap. They couldn't stand the taste of the lippet. They all said that the idea of using the lippet as breath fresheners made no sense, since they did not like the smell of their husband's breath after they had chewed on them.

"Was it always this way?" she asked the wives. "Have your husbands annoyed you this way for all of your time of marriage?"

Swov was the first to respond, after very little thought.

"No," she said. "The buds slowly became bitter. It happened very gradually. This started sometime after the Surati Plague."

"That's right," *Shao* agreed. "I did not really notice any problem until a while after the plague."

"That's exactly right!" *Karq* chimed in.

Tess asked to be shown to a bush that offered the buds. She broke one off and chewed on it.

"Yuck!" she said, and quickly spit it out. "It tastes like menthol chewing tobacco *smells*!"

There were no Corlan words for such a thing as menthol chewing tobacco, so she had used the English term.

Shao said, "Well, I don't know what 'menthol chewing tobacco' is, but if it's anything like this, then I would not like it."

Later on, at the evening meeting, *Tess* brought forth the second phase of her newest research project: abstinence from lippet.

"Gentlemen," she said, "there is some anecdotal evidence—and I have a strong intuition on it—that avoiding lippet may prolong your lives. I also tend to believe that the negative change to the telumni bush not only made the lippet detrimental to your health, but also the lippet may have become *habit forming*."

P'erry said, "You mean addictive? Like tensch juice?"

Everyone gasped.

"Yes," she said bluntly. "Like tensch juice."

"Oh, no!" Shao exclaimed. "Surely not!"

"Yes, sir," *Tess* argued, "Probably so."

"It cannot be!" Swov despaired.

"It most certainly can be, and likely is," *Tess* retorted.

"I cannot believe it," Karq announced.

"You'd better believe it," *Tess* said. "As of now you are all to abstain from lippet. You are probably going to suffer withdrawal symptoms. We all need to pray that the addiction, if there is one, is breakable."

Karq stood up. Then he sat down. Shao just sat in silence. Swov shook his head over and over.

Tess said, "I need to know how many lippet you have been chewing, and when."

"Two or three, after the evening meal," Karq said.

"Same here," Swov admitted.

Shao shamefully confessed, "Two or three after the morning meal; two or three more after lunch; and three or four after the evening meal."

Everyone gasped again.

Shao then pensively said, "I chewed five on the evening when I collapsed, the same night when P'erry had his conversion experience. I never put it together until now that the lippet could have caused the collapse."

Tess shook her head, pursed her lips with a look of determination, and then said, "You three gentlemen are addicted. Time will reveal whether or not this substance is detrimental. Any damage done may not be undoable, but we have to try. Uncle Karq and Uncle Swov, you are both moderately addicted. Uncle Shao, you are flat hooked. I'm of the opinion that this is going to be the toughest personal challenge you've ever faced."

They eschewed the lippet, starting with that very

evening's meal. They were surprised how soon the withdrawal symptoms started. Before they even made it to bed that night, they were dripping with sweat, craving the lippet, and becoming very grouchy. Shao suffered the most, with the broadest display of withdrawal symptoms.

"This is embarrassing! Humiliating!" he shouted to his family in private, and then he wept.

The next day, terrible headaches set in for all three, and Shao's skin crawled, itched, and burned.

For the next week, all three of them were horrendously grouchy, and several times they gave in and sneaked a little taste of lippet. Shao, who was the worst addict, gave in the most. Their wives slapped their hands, rebuked them, prayed over them, counseled them, and at one point, *Shao* even barred her husband from leaving their home.

In the second week, the withdrawal symptoms were reduced for Karq and Swov, but Shao suffered worse than ever.

In private, Shao lay before the Lord and cried out, "God, help me! You know that I was unwittingly ensnared in this pit. Please, spare me from this torment!"

The Lord answered him, but apparently Shao was not pleased with the reply. Shao seemed to settle in for a long, hard battle with the cravings, and he never told a soul—not Torreq, and not even his wife—what the Lord had said to him that day.

It was not that the Lord was punishing Shao. It was just that there were aspects of His plan that were beyond the understanding of His people.

By the fourth week, Shao was finally realizing some reduction of his cravings and symptoms. The three men, especially Shao, confessed that even after the symptoms wore off, they still suffered a strong mental compulsion to go back to the plant buds.

The overall experience had a profound emotional impact on the whole community, and especially on Shao. There was a renewed desperation to get to the New Land. Shao longed with all of his heart to get his people home to a proper paradise, to get all things back to the way they were supposed to be.

Everyone worked even longer hours than before. The hard work and lack of sufficient rest were hard on them, although not as hard as the lippet had been on the three men. During the marathon of hard weeks that followed, everyone aged dramatically except for the six youths and Daniel and *Tess*.

Tess' renewed greenhouse efforts finally produced a meager harvest of pure lithune, but the damage done by the contaminated food was not completely overcome, and still the aging continued. It was especially bad for those who had spent several denicam abusing the altered, terrible lippet.

◆◆◆◆◆◆◆

P'erry developed a wonderful routine of communicating with J'etsu every night, just before prayers and bedtime. J'etsu's keen sense of humor and charming laughter entertained, encouraged, and delighted P'erry. Their ability to communicate grew even stronger. It had always been instantaneous (no time lag), but now it was clearer than before, and more than just plenary (word-based) communication. They became able to project mental images—visual thoughts—in addition to their voices.

At the heart of their quickly growing friendship was a sense that they would always be a blessing to each other. P'erry was aware of the privilege of having a type of friendship that no other Human had ever had. Some aspects of their friendship were beyond the comprehension of those who had never experienced such a thing. He was overwhelmed with gratitude. Whereas he once hated his life on Sset and pitied himself for being raised there, he now appreciated it more than anything. He thanked God often.

Eventually P'erry went and asked Uncle Shao, "Why did none of the other Corlan ever enter into a friendship like this with a Tirran? Don't they know what they're missing?"

Uncle Shao slowly said, "Early on, I tried to explain it. I tried to encourage them to go and do as I had done, but there was a crucial difference between them and me. I never had any prior ancestor give me memories. From the very first child, all our Corlan children have had the memories handed to them. The memories are something they have experienced that you and I never have, and probably you never will.

"Through the memories, my children all gained a sweet comfort, as well as a deep sense of companionship and context. You and I cannot really understand it, just as they cannot really understand our bond with our Tirran friends. My children dwell in a serene place of continual solace. It fulfills them such that they never had any need to befriend a Tirra. So, they simply smiled whenever I tried to tell them about it. They smiled, but they never acted. I learned to accept that.

"You may find your children to be different. Only God above knows, and He does not always tell us all the mysteries that the future holds. After all, what would be the fun in knowing all the secrets of the future? I sometimes consider that, at times, knowing the end from the beginning might be dreadful for the Lord. I can just envision him sometimes hiding from his ability to know the future and be in the future by focusing on his relationship with us in the *now*.

"Can you imagine how frustrating it must be for Him when we are too distracted to commune with Him? I sometimes worry that my children don't take time to hear His voice like I do. I wonder if they pray only out of duty, instead of soaking up the precious, wonderful companionship of a considerate, compassionate Creator who longs for nothing more than to be with His creation in the *now*."

At that moment, Shao began to cough terribly, and blood began to drip from his mouth.

"Oh, no!" P'erry cried out. "Help! Someone help!"

Shao came running. She began to weep, as blood continued to pour from her husband's mouth, and he coughed up more and more of a dark, lumpy evidence of something gone terribly wrong inside his lungs.

Outside Shao's home, everyone was gathered in a prayer vigil for him, and only Daniel, *Tess*, *Shao* and *C'lou* were inside with him. Then Daniel and *Tess* came out to address the group.

Tess said somberly, "The appearance and texture of the lumps he is coughing up lead us to conclude that some *carcinogen* has been at work. It was probably the lippet."

Because the Corlan had never experienced cancer, they had no words for concepts such as carcinogen or cancer, so *Tess* had used an English word. It was a sad chapter in the Corlan history when such words had to be introduced into their vocabulary from English.

"What is a carcinogen?" Tap calmly asked.

"It is any substance or energy that, when ingested or absorbed, causes damage to the genetic 'building plan' inside of a person—the information necessary for life, functioning in the cells within the body. The damage can cause the body's cells to malfunction. Often, in such a confused state, the cells begin to multiply at an enormous rate, causing lumps—masses of tissue—where they ought not be. The damaged cells also can cease from fulfilling their intended function. The affected cells, the lumps, and all the other detrimental effects are collectively called *cancer*. Cancer can cause death. It often does."

Tap said, "These are terrible words to learn, and this is a sad knowledge to carry."

Daniel said, "I urge you to continue in prayer for Shao, back at your homes. The Lord is able to heal. If a miracle is not granted, however, Shao will likely die either sooner or later. The evidence we have seen indicates sooner."

Shao was bedfast. His wife was seldom seen as she cared for him continually. The illness made the people more determined than ever to finish the ship. They all worked even harder than before. Increased hours meant that sleep was taken in minimum doses. The stress of sleep deprivation pushed everyone toward grumpiness—everyone except Daniel and Tess, who, as glorified immortals, did not sleep. They two had been working on the shipbuilding project almost nonstop (both day and night) for quite some time.

Everyone sought to keep himself well-disciplined in

the midst of sleep-deprivation. There were very few arguments. In those moments when one of the Corlan would occasionally snap or make a harsh demand of another, the measured reply would begin, "For Shao...." The tears that were shed could not be counted.

Finally, they got the new ship completed. Considering the tiny size of their population, and their limited resources, it was a monumental undertaking and therefore a tremendous success. To float her, they slowly laid down a watergate, unleashing seawater previously pumped out of the shipyard. There was an understandable anxiety about whether she would have any leaks, and if so, how many. Yet an even greater concern silently nagged each of them. Was it too late? It was something all thought and none said.

They were pleased to see that, upon her initial float high in the water, there were no leaks.

Tap said, "We must weigh the ship down and see if there are leaks higher up. It must hold the weight of all the food and supplies, the baby animals, and all of us."

The food stores and animals were all loaded. The ship settled lower and lower into the water as the weight of each item or creature was added. No leaks were yet found.

Finally, it was time for all the people to board, to do the final leak check. Shao was near death, but he insisted that they carry him aboard. He was determined to not die on the land. He directed for them to not delay the launch because of waiting for him to die before the trip. They had obediently prepared his cabin to accommodate his bedfast condition. Everyone was immensely grateful that they had named both the new ship and the earlier one after him. They carried him onto the ship, and got him settled in his new quarters. There were no leaks!

They planned for a final night of rest in their homes, followed by an early morning departure. The Shao family was to spend the night on the ship, rather than have Shao suffer two more tiresome moves—from the ship to their house and back in the morning.

That last evening on land, P'erry anxiously waited at home for contact from J'etsu.

"Hello, my puny friend," came the standard greeting at last.

"Hello, my huge friend," P'erry responded. "I have important news. Tonight is our last night on land. Early tomorrow we will sail onto the ocean, trying to get to the New Land. We don't know how long it will take. We are trusting God to help us."

There was no reply for a while. At first P'erry felt that J'etsu was simply thinking, but eventually he became concerned that his thoughts had not been heard.

"Did you hear me?"

"Yes, I'm sorry," J'etsu said quickly. "I was wondering to myself whether we would be able to talk while you are sailing across the ocean."

"I was worried about the same thing," P'erry said. After another pause, he asked, "Do you think you could ask Torreq if he and Shao were able to talk during the last voyage?"

"Great idea," J'etsu said. "I will ask him."

After a time of silence that seemed to P'erry like far too long of a delay, J'etsu spoke again.

"Torreq said that they did talk during the last voyage. He used the moving window that I told you about to find and keep track of the ship. He said it was hard sometimes, but he was able to do it. He also used the moving window to find the New Land, so he could help Shao to know the way."

"Shao knew the direction to the New Land?" P'erry asked.

"Yes," the Tirra answered, "but neither of them knew how long it would take to get there. In the end, it was much farther than the first ship could go."

P'erry was amazed to learn that the Tirran ability to use a "moving window" could serve such a purpose.

"That is so amazing," he finally sent.

"What?"

"That the moving window can be used in that way."

"I am sorry that I cannot explain it better. If you spoke my language it would be much easier. Corlan words are not the same as Tirran language."

"Can you teach me your language?" P'erry asked.

"I don't think so. I think it is not something you are even capable of."

"OK," P'erry said, using the ancient English term. The Corlan people had heard P'erry's family use the same word, and some of them had even started using it occasionally. However, since it was not classical Corlan, J'etsu did not understand it.

"What is O—K?"

"That's an Earth word my parents taught me."

"What does it mean?"

"Umm. I guess it means a lot of things. It can mean good, or great, or acceptable, or alright, or 'meaning understood,' or… a bunch of things."

"Will you teach me the history of this word? I want to know the story behind it."

"I don't know. I will ask."

Tess came near and said, "Time for prayers. You need a good night's sleep. You have a long day tomorrow."

"Yes, ma'am," P'erry said. "Hey, Mom, what's the history behind the word *OK?*"

Her answer was littered with many English words that had no Corlan alternative, and which P'erry himself barely understood.

"A long time ago on Earth, long before your father and I were born, there was a presidential campaign in the United States of America. One of the candidates running for President was named Martin Van Buren. His nickname was Old Kinderhook. He was called O.K. for short. Whenever his supporters asked other citizens if they were planning to vote for Old Kinderhook, the question was sometimes posed as 'Are you for O.K.?'"

"The answers were deemed acceptable if they responded with O.K. as the favored candidate. This led to 'I'm for O.K.' or 'I'm O.K.' Eventually the idea was established that being on the side of O.K. was the right side to be on, because O.K. was supposedly good for the nation. This led to a new word for 'good' or meaning 'on the right side' of things."

"Oh," P'erry said. "Wow. I don't think I will be able to explain that."

P'erry then sent these words to J'etsu, using English terms where necessary, "A long time ago in the United States of America, there was once an election for President—"

"Wait," J'etsu said. "What is 'statesofamerica'? What is president?"

"Umm," P'erry paused, considering how difficult it would be to explain, when every word explained would lead to many others that would need to be explained. "I don't think I can teach you English. Maybe it is not something you are even capable of."

J'etsu conveyed that he was rolling with laughter.

"What's so funny?" P'erry asked.

"You are so funny," J'etsu explained. "You gave me the same answer I gave you. We are funny, you and I. At least we can both speak Corlan. I am glad of that."

"Yes," P'erry said. "That is good. It is OK. Say 'OK.'"

"I am not used to saying any word whose history is unknown. Tirra don't speak that way, but I will do this for you. It is OK. I am glad, so it is OK."

P'erry laughed. J'etsu chortled. Their laughter came through the thought-based communication as an emotional presentation, more of a feeling than a sound.

P'erry shouted, both aloud so his parents could hear, and via thought for J'etsu, "It is OK!"

"What's OK, dear?" asked his mother.

"OK is OK!"

She raised her eyebrows and then wrinkled one brow downward in confusion.

"OK," she muttered with a tone of curiosity.

J'etsu laughed on.

Daniel led the little family in prayer, and then P'erry went to bed. He was asleep practically before his head hit the pillow.

That night he dreamed of bubbles.

His parents, as immortals who never sleep, spent the night in glorious communion with the Spirit of God, except for a time when *Tess* updated her astronomical charts of the progress of the other moons orbiting T'and.

The morning arrived slowly, as it did every day on Sset, with the gradual brightening and widening of the trasedondi (glow strip) above. As always, it was a crisp, beautiful day.

"Up and at it, son!" Daniel called to his son.

Weeks on end without enough sleep made it very difficult for P'erry to wake up. His head and neck ached, and his eyelids felt weighty.

"Come on, P'erry!" his father called again. "We're burning daylight!"

"Ohhh," P'erry groaned as he swung his feet onto the floor. "What does that even mean?"

Then he remembered what day it was. Excitement washed away the weariness, replacing it with enthusiasm. Within minutes he had dressed and eaten, and they made their way down to where the ship was docked.

As they boarded the vessel, they were greeted by the Corlan already on board. Everyone was there except the Swov family, which arrived shortly afterward.

Tap led everyone in prayer before the launch. They prayed for God's help, for smooth seas, fast winds, and success in their journey. Then they got to work.

When the sails were unfurled, they quickly filled with air, and the huge ship's progress was swift and uneventful. The journey had begun.

◆◆◆◆◆◆◆

P'erry and the two other young men were assigned to take turns serving as the barrelman (the lookout). During each one's shift, he was stationed in the masthead (also called the crow's nest), which was a small platform partway up the mast, just above the height of the mast's main yard (sail). (Back on Earth, the barrelman was the fellow most likely to be heard shouting, "Land, Ahoy!") R'ei was to take the first shift.

P'erry and T'anah worked to help the adults on the main deck. After a flurry of initial activity, they eventually got everything handled, and things calmed down. As everyone settled in, conversations began here and there.

C'lou found P'erry talking with T'anah on the main deck. The two young men interrupted their conversation to ask about her father. She stared out at the mainland that was slowly fading into the distance, and her beautiful eyes were profoundly sad.

"My father is dying," she said somberly. "He does not have much time. It seems clear that God's plan is to allow this to happen. I cannot fully understand this. Everything my father has taught me says to trust God no matter what. That has been his counsel both in person and via my mother's memories of him. Yet I find that nothing has prepared me for this."

P'erry ached inside when he saw her sorrow. He felt helpless. Then he remembered something.

"You should talk to my mother," P'erry finally advised. "She lost both her father *and* mother to death when she was only a couple of denicam older than you are. Back on Earth, there was no such thing as surati, so she didn't even have the comfort of prior memories. If you talk to her, she might be able to help you through this."

As he spoke, she turned her eyes toward him, while still facing the slowly disappearing coastline. With a degree of maturity that was impressive for her age, she realized that what *Tess* had suffered made her plight seem smaller by comparison, and just knowing what *Tess* had endured helped her somehow. Realizing what God had eventually done through *Tess* and seeing what she had become for Him gave *C'lou* hope and faith for the future, even while the present circumstances seemed too painful to endure.

"I will talk to her," she said with determination. "Thank you, P'erry."

She turned to go and find *Tess*. P'erry turned back to T'anah, whose eyes were turned down in a frown, and there was a tightlipped anger on his face.

"What's wrong?" P'erry asked cautiously.

T'anah shook his head, and said, "Everything. Everything is wrong. This is all the work of the Ettosedondi. His curse is upon us all! If he can reach out from beyond death and kill our Eldest, how are any of us safe? It is a terrible thing what he did. It is a terror how his evil deed has ruined everything for our whole kind."

Daniel had come up behind the two boys. He had heard most of what T'anah said. "Sin is a nasty thing," he said. "It almost never damages only the one who sins. Back on Earth, the first Human's sin brought a terrible curse upon all the Humans born afterward—billions of them, including me, *Tess*, and P'erry.

"Here on Sset, the Ettosedondi's sin has caused pain and suffering for everyone, and death for most. However, since he was not the first Corlan—not the Eldest—perhaps God will not allow his curse to continually damage all those who have not knowingly sinned. Our hope is that when we reach the New Land, you will finally be free from the reach of the Ettosedondi's sin."

T'anah looked up to Daniel and said, "I pray it is so."

C'lou found *Tess,* and despite her determination not to, she burst into tears as she said, "*Aunt Tess*, my father is dying. My heart is breaking. I confess that I'm struggling to trust God through this. Has my father sinned? If he has not sinned, why is God refusing to spare him from the death caused by lippet? This does not seem right. It does not seem fair to punish my whole kind for just one Corlan's sin."

Tess noticed *Tap* passing by and motioned for her.

"*C'lou,* when you're young one of the things you lack is proper perspective. Now, because of the memories you've been getting from your mother, you're probably twice as mature at your age as I was at the same age. You remember not only your 14 denicam of living, but also many denicam from your mother's life. Yet the portion of her memories that you have so far is but a very short time compared to how long she has lived.

"Your mother is facing a much more grievous prospect for the future, and she is enduring much greater suffering. Yet she is facing it with strength—not only because of her faith, but also because of the sense of perspective she has gained over hundreds of cam.

Also, consider *Tap*. She lost *both* of her parents after having them around her for hundreds of cam. She is handling the sorrow and grief with strength. So are Karq and Swov, who lost both of their parents too. Part of the reason for their strength is faith in God, and faith in God's word, particularly the promise He has given to the Corlan about the resurrection of the righteous. However, another reason is because of the sense of perspective you gain over time.

"Everything seems overly magnified when you are young. In the grand scheme of things, I suspect we will eventually find out that God's plan for your father, and for your mother, is much greater than just raising him up from this sickness now. By faith, I can promise you that even if your father dies from this sickness, you will one day be with him again, and then it will be better than you can even imagine right now."

C'lou nodded and leaned on her cousin, *Tap*.

Tap held her, and said, "I don't know when, or how it will happen, but I am trusting God that I will see my mother and father again; not only them, but also many of our people who faced death so nobly and without sin."

C'lou said, "*Aunt Tess*, how do you think this might happen? What will it be like?"

"I don't know. I'm the wrong person to ask. The one you should be asking is the Lord. Perhaps one of His reasons for this trial is to strengthen your relationship with Him. Ever stop to think about why you let all these questions pile up and then came to me, instead of going to Him?"

C'lou hung her head. Then she looked up and smiled.

"I will ask the Lord my questions. I will listen to Him for the answers."

That night P'erry lay in his bunk in the men's area and waited for word from J'etsu. It never came.

"Come on, J'etsu," he said to himself, "find us with that movable window."

That same night in her bunk, *C'lou* prayed. The presence of the Lord came to her. In the comfort of His company, there was a peace that somehow made the answers unnecessary. She drifted off to sleep. She dreamed of a place of pure joy, where there were many Corlan. Some she knew. Most she did not.

In that place, she went looking for her father. Everywhere she asked, the people pointed her onward. She finally entered a beautiful room. Again she asked for her father. Someone pointed toward a man seated on an impressive, ornate seat. He glowed with light and glory. As she approached the throne, the man rose to meet her. As she drew near, she realized He was not Shao; this was the Lord Himself. Before she reached Him, the dream ended. An overwhelming joy lingered after she finally awoke.

Morning. Back on the ship. The endless motion of the waves rocking the vessel. She suddenly missed the place where she had just been, with a sweet pain that cannot be described.

She dressed quickly and then ran to her father, but he was still sleeping. She waited by his side until finally, in a terrible fit of coughing, he awoke. *Shao* stood near.

C'lou said, "Father, I've just seen where you are going. It is beautiful beyond words. Your children are there—all the righteous who died in faith. I've seen *the* Father. The Lord. I almost got to Him before the vision ended."

"I've seen it too," he confided. "My only regret is not being here with my wife, you, and the others. I trust that the Lord has a plan. Somehow there will be a way."

◆◆◆◆◆◆◆

All day, their second at sea, P'erry hoped for word from J'etsu. Nothing. That afternoon, he had the last shift in the crow's nest. As he took his turn, he watched, waited, and prayed. Nothing.

"Come on, J'etsu," he pleaded over and over, "please find us."

As his shift in the crow's nest ended, he began to despair over the possibility of not hearing from J'etsu ever again. He gathered that using the movable window and finding a relatively small ship on the huge, open ocean would be tougher than "finding a needle in a haystack." (That was a phrase his parents had sometimes used.) P'erry climbed down and headed for his bunk.

Suddenly an excited voice projected into his mind, "Hello, my puny friend! I found you!"

"Hello, my huge friend! I am *so* glad you did!"

"Yes. Everything is good now."

"What happened? Did you lose track of the ship?"

"Yes," J'etsu answered. "It seems I needed to allow for the time difference between morning on the mainland and morning here on the island. By the time I checked for you that morning, your ship had already departed. I've been searching ever since. I finally found you some time ago. I tried to contact you before now, but I could not open the window inside your sedondi like usual. I kept trying and trying, the whole time you were alone at the top of the ship. I could see you sitting on the top, but I could not reach you. After you climbed down, I was able to reach you."

"So, the movable window loses power if I am off the ground?"

"I don't know. I don't see why that would matter."

P'erry said, "J'etsu, I am so glad you found us. Please do your best not to lose us again. If I find out that we're going to change course, I will do my best to let you know in advance."

That night, P'erry slept soundly.

After three days on the open sea, in the evening, Tap came up and summoned Daniel, *Tess*, and P'erry.

"I fear that the Eldest is passing from us," he said. "He is calling for you."

Some of the Corlan were gathered close around him. They made way for Daniel, *Tess*, and P'erry to come in close. The rest of the Corlan were summoned, and they came in quickly. Shao was colorless, and he could hardly breathe. His voice was rough and barely a whisper.

"I love you all. Thank you for all you have done," he said, and then he turned to P'erry. "My young friend, I love you. You are truly Corlan. Just as much as any of my precious children, you are truly Corlan. P'erry—"

More of the coughing of blood warned them of the nearness of the hour.

With some struggle, Shao continued, "Perry, the Lord

has spoken to me again. It is the same as before. You are the key. He has given you the answer. You need only to see what is in front of you. See what is obvious."

P'erry suddenly knew that it involved having J'etsu use the movable window to help, just as Shao had help from Torreq, so he answered with confidence.

"Yes, sir," he said. "I will find the way."

Shao looked toward everyone and said, "Be strong, and of good courage. The Lord is with you. You are going to make it to the New Land. Tap, you are the leader now. I love you all. I love you...."

Those were his last words.

The Eldest Corlan was dead.

On an island not all that far in front of them, the Eldest Tirran, Torreq, roared so loudly that every Tirran heard it. He was mourning the passing of his dear friend.

On the ship, the people wept.

Aunt Shao went to a box at the foot of the bed and withdrew her husband's ancient coat. It was one of the oldest garments in existence. The distinctive cloak had become synonymous with Shao, and spoke of his authority as the Eldest. She carried it to Tap, and then she placed the mantle about his shoulders.

"Lead this people, my son," she said firmly.

Tap buried his head his mother's arms and wailed in agony.

Chapter VIII

Reunion and Parting

Tap said to Daniel, "In our prior voyage, we were four days out when we came to land. It was one of the island homes of the Tirra. I am hoping for that land again, because I greatly desire for us to bury our father there. It seems clear that he did not wish to be buried in the Old Land. I don't think we should turn back just to bury his body there."

Daniel said, "Shao does not want us to turn back. But do you think our moon charts will help us now? The ones we made on the prior voyage were hastily drawn, and we're sailing at a different time during the cam. The moons' locations are different. It would take some very complex calculations to find that island again. My wife has some newer charts, but they are rather incomplete. If we miss the island, are you opposed to a burial at sea?"

"I'm not utterly opposed, but it would grieve me."

As they studied the moon charts from the previous voyage, Daniel said, "Well, I will go get *Tess*. She may be able to help."

Daniel found *Tess* and asked, "In our first voyage, we came to an island about four days out. Any chance you could extrapolate the location of that island, based on its relationship to the locations of the moons then and now?"

She said, "Whew! That's going to be tough, but I will try. Although I've been studying the other moons' orbits ever since the first voyage, I'm a long way from ascertaining their orbital eccentricity, periods, arguments of periapsis, longitudes of ascending nodes, and on and on. We really need...."

Both Daniel's and *Tess'* eyes widened as they thought of the same solution simultaneously.

"We need a Tirra!" they both said.

"I'll get P'erry," Daniel said.

It was P'erry's shift to serve as the barrelman. Daniel asked R'ei if he would cover for P'erry. R'ei was glad to be relieved of his tiresome job helping on the main deck. R'ei climbed up, and P'erry climbed down.

Both Daniel and J'etsu began to speak to P'erry at the same time. It surprised him, and it was so confusing to him that he could not understand either one of them.

"Wait," he said, as he raised both his hands. "One at a

time. Dad, can you say that again?"

His father said, "P'erry, if and when you get any contact from J'etsu, we need to know it. We need his help."

"Yes, sir," P'erry replied. "I have good news. J'etsu is in contact with me right now."

"Excellent. Come with me to the navigation deck."

P'erry projected to J'etsu, "What were you starting to say to me just now?"

J'etsu sent back, "I have been trying to contact you while you were on top of the ship. For some reason, while you were alone, I could not make the window work inside your sedondi. However, as soon as the other boy climbed up to where you were, I was able to get the window to work. I did not want to contact you while you were climbing down, because I did not want to risk making you fall. I just kept chasing you with the window. As you were climbing down, the window stopped working again, for a while. As soon as you got near to your father, I was able to contact you again."

"So, the window does not work inside my sedondi unless someone is near me?" P'erry asked.

"It seems so, although I don't see why that should matter."

"I might know," P'erry said. He was thinking of bubbles.

Just then they arrived where *Tess* and Tap were waiting on the navigation deck.

P'erry dared to guess at what they needed.

"So, you need me to get J'etsu to locate the New Land, right?"

Tess said, "P'erry, that's not what we were going to ask, but what makes you say that?"

P'erry was confused somewhat, but he said, "I found out from Torreq, through J'etsu, that a Tirra can control a 'movable window'—as they call it—and use it to find things. Before J'etsu can talk to me from a distance, he must first find me with the movable window. During the prior voyage, when Shao was navigating, he was getting help from Torreq, because Torreq had located the New Land. Shao knew which way to go. He just did not know how far away the New Land was."

There was silence for several seconds, during which only the sound of the ocean and the noise of the wind in the sails were heard.

Finally, Daniel shouted, "Woo-hoo! This is better than we had hoped for!"

"That's excellent news, son," *Tess* said with a smile.

Tap said, "Excellent, indeed! But first we need to be guided to the island that is nearest us. We think it is about a day from here. It is one of the Tirran islands. We need to bury our father."

"Yes, sir," P'erry said, "I understand, Uncle Tap."

Then to his big friend, P'erry sent, "J'etsu, I have bad news. The Corlan Eldest has died."

"We are aware of this. Our Eldest knew it as it happened."

"Well, we need to get to the Tirran island nearest to us. We need to bury the Corlan Eldest."

"O—K— That will be easy. Tell them to turn the ship's direction to their right hand side, until I tell them to straighten."

P'erry smiled at J'etsu's use of the word OK, and then he relayed the message to the patiently waiting adults, who had been unable to hear a word of the telepathic conversation.

"J'etsu says it's no problem. Actually, he said 'OK.' I taught him that. He says to steer the ship toward the starboard, until he tells us to straighten our course."

As *Tess* and Daniel hugged P'erry, Tap smiled with relief and turned the wheel that controlled the ship's rudder. The ship leaned slightly as it turned.

"Straighten now!" J'etsu signaled.

"Straighten now!" P'erry relayed.

"Done," Tap confirmed, as he wheeled the ship onto a straightened path.

Daniel said, "Well son, I guess you should stay here, in case we need to make any more course corrections. Have you been talking very much with J'etsu while you were up in the crow's nest?"

P'erry answered, "Well, Dad, about that; J'etsu has figured out that whenever I am alone, he cannot talk to me.

He can only talk to me while someone else is with me or near me."

Daniel said, "You're kidding, right?"

P'erry said, "No, sir. That's really how it is."

"You don't say!" Daniel said. "Now that is interesting."

Tess said, "That is very interesting, indeed."

For the next few minutes, J'etsu sent occasional course corrections, while he and P'erry laughed as Daniel tried to explain to them about radio-controlled model ships on Earth, and how the HMS Shao II was now like a huge, remotely controlled ship, possibly the largest in the history of two universes.

Suddenly, they heard a voice yelling from a distance. It was R'ei calling down from the crow's nest. Everyone thought they faintly heard his voice shouting, "Land!"

Tap said, "Could it be that we have arrived early?"

They had arrived early. The winds had been stronger than during their previous journey, and the huge ship had made even better time than its smaller counterpart from before.

At dusk, a welcoming squadron of Tirra appeared overhead, led by Torreq. J'etsu was among them. He was the only Tirran youth permitted to be in the delegation. Everyone stood out on the main deck, and P'erry waved to his friend.

Shao said quietly, "My husband almost got to see his

dear friend, Torreq, one last time. If he had just lived a few more hours."

When they got near enough to the island, they furled the sails and anchored the ship. Finally everyone met together. It was decided that they would get a good night's sleep, and then go ashore the next morning.

That night P'erry tossed and turned in his bunk. He had wanted to visit with J'etsu right away, and the disappointment of not getting to, combined with the excitement of being so close to the island, left him wide eyed.

Meanwhile, *C'lou* tossed and turned in her bunk on the other side of the ship. She wanted to sleep so badly that she couldn't sleep. She hoped to be granted another dream of the place that she had visited previously, where she saw the Lord. She longed to go to sleep, and via a dream from God, perhaps get to see her father after his arrival there because of his passing. *C'lou* finally slipped into what was, sadly, a dreamless sleep.

Some time later, P'erry eventually fell asleep, and he restlessly dreamed of again flying on J'etsu's back. It was not a dream from God. It was just a dream. At one point during the dream, his face rolled into his pillow, making it difficult for him to breathe. His subconscious alerted him inside the dream by having J'etsu fly too high. Distorted memories—of blacking out and suffering the broken arm—crept into the dream and shattered it. He woke up and rolled his face away from the pillow. It took a long time for him to get back to sleep.

When the ship's bell rang in the morning, P'erry reluctantly awoke to face a hectic whirlwind of activity all around him. His neck ached again, and his eyes burned.

"Ohh," he moaned. "I have got to get some more sleep sometime." Then he remembered where they were, and he added, "But not today!"

Daniel noticed that P'erry was leaning his head from side to side, trying to stretch his neck muscles. His father pulled him close, facing P'erry's back, and he began to massage the sore, stiff muscles in P'erry's neck and shoulders. His fingers were like magic. As the pain and stiffness melted away, P'erry suddenly felt so loved by his parents that it overjoyed him. But, oh, how he would miss Uncle Shao.

"Dad," he asked, "do you know what they have planned for Uncle Shao's... *funeral?*" (He had to use the English word, funeral, because there is no such word in the Corlan language.) "I keep thinking about the time when Mom told me about Professor Dunkirk's burial, and how she cried when the Marines honored his memory with the twenty-one-gun salute, and the folding of a flag, and the song, 'Taps.' It seems like we should plan to do something like that to honor him."

"I don't know what they have planned, son," Daniel said, "but that sounds like a great idea. We will talk to Tap about it. The surviving Corlan have practically no experience with funerals. I think the only one who has ever buried someone is Swov. His daughter, *Tav*, died at night while trying to carry *Z'aey* to Swov's house. That was when *Z'aey* was just an infant. We arrived not long after that. Swov said he simply buried her. There was not enough time or adequate security for anything more. This time needs to be different. We are safe, and we have the time. This was the Corlan Eldest. I hope they do have some sort of ceremony."

All around them, chores were being accomplished, and they had to break their conversation to start helping. The baby animals were all fed, and their stalls were cleaned. The wrapped body of Shao was placed into one of the little longboats, for transport to the island. Eventually, the people carefully climbed down into the longboats, one by one, and finally they rowed to shore.

A regal delegation of the Tirra met them on the shore. It was the same group that had greeted them from the sky the prior evening.

On the beach of white sand, P'erry ran to his friend and leaned into him, face first, with his arms wrapped as wide as he could get them across the Tirran youth's broad chest. As they greeted each other telepathically, Torreq and the members of the delegation greeted the others as well.

The island had several tall mountains, including one that was not far from the beach where they landed. From a cleft in that nearest mountain, a decent-size waterfall could be seen, pouring a significant amount of water into a river than ran down through the massive trees that shaded the edge of the beach. Several hundred ment to their left, that river reached the ocean.

Several—including Daniel, *Tess*, P'erry, and all of the Corlan youth—had not ever seen ancient trees that were untouched by the surati plague. They had never imagined that the tiny trees they had known on the mainland had the potential to grow so large. They were accustomed to seeing trees that were only a cam or so of age. The island trees were over 300 cam old.

The Tirra had harvested some fruits and vegetables from the island, just for the Corlan. None of it was the Tirran kind of food. Their salty food from the ocean was not palatable to the Corlan. The Tirra had carefully carried their Corlan-intended harvest and gathered it near the shore.

Tap led all the Corlan in bowing to the Tirran Eldest out of respect and to show gratitude for their gift. It was obvious that either wind or migration had carried contaminated pollen to the island. All the gathered food showed the dimples, lumps, and horns that indicated contamination. Yet even in its contaminated state, the produce was more nourishing than any food on Earth during the reign of sin.

The Tirra had also gathered some dried wood into a massive pile on the white beach, and Tap announced that a fire was to be lit there. He relayed that Torreq had told him that there would be a natural flame kept alive there for as long as the Tirra could maintain it, as a symbol to honor Shao, because a great light had been extinguished by his passing.

Before very long, everyone was either sitting or standing around the roaring fire, recounting memories of Shao. There were laughs, tears, cheers, and hugs.

Daniel leaned over to P'erry and said, "Back on Earth, we used to call this a 'wake' or a family visitation."

Daniel and *Tess* went and talked with Tap about the Corlan ideas and plans for a proper ceremony to honor Shao.

"Back on Earth," *Tess* told Tap, "we buried a lot of good people, a lot of genuine heroes. We are experts at it, more than anyone here on Sset. Now that the sin of the Ettosedondi has brought death into this world, let us counsel you on how a *funeral* ceremony can help you and your people heal—emotionally and spiritually—after such a death. Without such a ceremony, you might find that there would be an open-ended sense of loss, with no healthy sense of closure."

"Say on," Tap said. "We welcome your counsel."

C'lou sat gazing into the fire, lost in a sea of memories of her father. She was approached at various times by her adult siblings, cousins, and niece. All the conversations

145

were pleasant and helpful, but the words of her sister, *Karq*, and her niece, *Swov*, were the most beneficial. After each one moved on, she returned to her reverie, staring into the firelight. The only thing that distracted her was when she curiously noticed Tap, Daniel, and *Tess* gathering all the young men together and teaching them something regarding her father's cloak, the one that her mother had given to her brother, Tap.

As the evening drew on, before the light of the glow strip had completely faded, Tap called for everyone's attention. A huge company of Tirra covered the beach in all directions, surrounding the Corlan family that was gathered around the fire. Two Tirra flew out to the ship, and carefully landed on the main deck. There, they waited silently. The words on the beach were being relayed to them telepathically.

Shao's wrapped body was hand carried by the Corlan "pallbearers" (Karq, T'anah, Swov, R'ei, Daniel, and P'erry) to a rock outcropping visible within the fire's light. Once they laid him there, *Tap* came near and spread the Eldest one's cloak over his lifeless form. It was that same ancient mantle that *Shao* had given to Tap earlier.

In spite of Tap's gray hair and age, he stood straight and tall. He spoke with a strength that warranted the burden of leadership that Shao had, in his final act, bestowed upon the last living Elder of the Council.

"The Corlan family, and our Tirran extended family," he began, "are gathered to give due honor and respect to the greatest, most valiant man we have ever known. God formed our father, Shao—the first of our kind—from the soil of the new world at the dawn of time. As God's appointed and benevolent leader, our father ruled over this world for 313 cam, until his death today. I humbly stand in his place, to declare that he can never be replaced. There will never be another like him."

Tess quickly tallied the total and whispered to Daniel, "That would be about 3,035 Earth years!"

Tap continued, "Shao saw 26 C'alimnet festivals during his life, and accordingly he fathered 26 children by our First Mother. During that time his offspring married and produced some 61,000 or so grandchildren. Only three of his first-generation children now remain, and our entire Corlan family now numbers only 15."

Tap said the last part with a twinkle in his eye and a nod toward the little family from Earth. When Tap had said 15, instead of 12, it was because he was counting Daniel, *Tess*, and P'erry as being part the Corlan family.

Tap went on, "Our father's lifetime—barely over three pascam—was all too short. He that should have been an ageless wonder of God's creation was cut off from the living far too soon. To mark the precious ages of his life, we will now toll the ship's bell three times, once for each pascam."

A reverent silence followed, during which the popping and cracking sounds from the fire were all that could be heard. Suddenly the sound of the bell pierced the air like a shot. The harmony of its ringing had never sounded sorrowful until that moment, yet it would forever afterward be a thing somewhat associated with sadness. There were three loud tolls, and each echoed off the mountain, and back out to sea.

Tap wept silently, and then cleared his throat and continued, with a voice breaking only occasionally, "During our leader's life, great advancements were made in the arts and sciences, including the areas of physics, mechanics, mathematics, and so on. The great zenith of Corlan accomplishment seen prior to the coming of the Ettosedondi testifies to the great potential that God imbued into our precious father. Even flight was achieved in a limited, mechanical sense.

"However, if he were here now, he would confess that mechanical flight was not his greatest dream. The only dream our father left unfulfilled was that of flying on the back of his friend, the Tirran Eldest, Torreq. At this word, I now give way for Torreq to speak, through my nephew Swov."

Torreq and Swov both stepped forwarded. Torreq let out an audible, mournful sound that P'erry never forgot. Then there was a pause, while Torreq communicated with Swov. Finally Swov began to echo the words.

"My dear friend loved me, and I loved him. Our friendship never competed with our love for our wives, or for our children, and our friendship cannot rightfully be compared with any other loves in our life. There is one glory of the sky, and another glory of the ground. There is another glory of the moons, and yet another glory of the trasedondi.

"Just as those differing glories cannot rightfully be compared among one another, so also, the various loves in our lives cannot be compared among one another. Our mutual love, friendship, and fellowship were wonderful for the two fathers of our two kinds to share. I shall mourn his passing every day, hoping for a day when I can see him again. Until that day, my dearest sympathies and most heartfelt prayers are for his wife, who faces a future dimmed by this loss. May God help and comfort you, dear, precious one."

Swov glanced at Torreq and nodded. Then they both stepped back.

Tap resumed speaking, "While our father never flew on the back of a Tirra, one among us dared to fulfill such a dream and lived to tell of it. At this word, I now give way for P'erry to come, along with T'anah and R'ei, to conduct the ceremony of the passing of the mantle."

P'erry blinked away the tears, and did his best to hold onto his composure. The other two boys faced the same struggle. With as much dignity as they could afford, they approached Shao's body, walking as though they were Marines at attention.

T'anah slowly and carefully took hold of the top of the cloak, at Shao's head, and P'erry likewise took hold of the bottom of it, at Shao's feet. They stepped away from the body and the rock outcropping, and spread the distance between themselves, pulling the garment out taut and straight. R'ei slowly and ceremoniously gathered the parts hanging down on either side, and folded them up onto the middle that was suspended between the other two boys.

Like a Marine folding a flag, P'erry then did his best to fold up the cloak from the bottom, creeping toward T'anah by tiny steps. While the boys were not nearly as perfect as the skillful Marines of Earth's past, they performed the ceremony with all their hearts, and they did well, considering how little practice they had.

As they finished folding the cloak, *Aunt Shao* walked up, and stood between them and Tap. The three boys turned to face her.

With a breaking voice, P'erry said, "All our love, *Aunt Shao*, and all our prayers."

Shao turned to Tap. She handed him the folded mantle, and then she spoke loud and clear.

"Tap, you are the last living male out of all our 26 first-generation children, and you are the last living Elder who served on the Council. You were chosen by your father, the Eldest, and appointed by him before he died to lead this people and to rule this world. I charge you before God and this assembly to rule well, to lead with integrity, and to finish what your father began."

Then she turned from Tap to face the others.

She spoke more loudly as she addressed the entire gathering, "Let it be known by all our Tirran friends, and throughout all of Sset, that although Shao is gone, this world is not without a leader. I charge you to hear and to heed, to honor and to obey this man, Tap, with the same reverence and loyalty you granted unto his father."

She turned back to Tap and said, "Lead this people, my son. Lead them to the New Land, as your father directed. Rule this world well. God will be with you. May you live forever in peace and prosperity."

Something in her tone seemed to somehow convey a hint of a goodbye, and Tap caught it. He searched his mother's eyes for a clue that he might have missed. She saw his perplexity, and she smiled it away.

As she stepped away, Tap nodded to Torreq. Without any uttered sound, Torreq signaled the two Tirra on the ship. They launched themselves into the air and soared toward the shore, gaining altitude as they approached. Torreq stepped forward, leaned his long neck down, and laid his head against Shao's body. Then he crouched, leaped into the air, and flew over the crowd before looping back toward the location of the fire.

The two Tirra from the ship flew over the heads of the crowd and on toward the mountain. They landed on either side of the waterfall, and each reached into the flow of water with one of their wings. They linked their extended wings together, and the flow of water was diverted across their wings and then across their bodies. They had opened up a doorway in the waterfall. A hidden cave opening was revealed behind the waterfall.

Torreq had looped back, and now he was coming down slowly, flapping hard in what was almost a hover. He reached with his back feet, and grabbed Shao's body. Once he had a good hold on his dear friend's former home, he carefully elevated himself, lifting the corpse as he went. Then he flew to the cave, and deposited Shao's body inside. As he flew back toward the crowd, the other two Tirra removed their wings, releasing the flow of the waterfall. Then they leaped into the air, and joined their Eldest in flying back toward the shore.

After the three Tirra had returned to the shore, Tap said, "With this burial completed, I now give way for Talbot and *Talbot* to come, to pray for God's help and blessing upon us all, and to conclude this ceremony."

Daniel and *Tess* looked at each other because of Tap's use of their ancient last name from their days of being married back on Earth. It was the first time anyone on Sset had publicly referred to them by their old "one name." It was somehow very "Corlan" and very fitting for the first Corlan burial ceremony after the Surati Plague.

They stepped forward. Daniel squeezed *Tess'* hand to signal for her to go first, so that he could wrap up things with his conclusion, before the song finale.

Tess prayed, "Dear Lord, we speak for an entire world when we say thank you for the precious leader you gave in Shao. Thank you for each and every day of his life, through times of good and times of evil. Each moment with him was a blessing. He led with honor, wisdom, and sensitivity to your Spirit. He always obeyed the guidance You gave. At his passing, the light of the Corlan people is gone out, yet because of his godly leadership, the light that *is* the Corlan people will never be extinguished. Thank you for great grace upon us."

Daniel said, "Although Shao's body is lifeless, we know his soul lives on. Even now he is with the Lord. A holy man of God back on Earth was once inspired to write, 'Therefore we are always confident and know that as long as we are at home in the body we are away from the Lord. We live by faith, not by sight. We are confident, I say, and would prefer to be away from the body and at home with the Lord.'

"The next time we see Shao... there will be no more cancer. He will be tall, strong, and whole. You will know him when you see him. I declare that which I know to be truth."

Daniel then squared his shoulders, lifted his head, and

loudly pronounced, "Since it has pleased our Heavenly Father in His wise providence to take unto Himself our beloved Shao, we therefore commit his body to the ground, soil to soil, ashes to ashes, and dust to dust, with blessed hope looking for the next glorious appearing of our great God and Savior. In accordance with the promise of our Lord, which was granted through the prophecy of Shao, we know that a resurrection awaits our friend, when the Lord shall quicken his body and fashion it anew, in the likeness of His own body of glory."

Daniel then looked at *Tess* and announced, "We will conclude the ceremony with a song."

Tess had long since memorized the lyrics to "Taps" back on Earth, and that evening on Sset she had been able to quickly translate the words into Corlan. The English version which follows is a loose translation of how she edited a couple of Earth-based references over to Sset-based references to make the haunting tune fitting for another world. She lifted up her voice and sang:

Day is done, gone trasedon'
From the lakes, from the hills, from the sky
All is well, safely rest
God is nigh.

Fading light dims the sight
And the moons gem the sky, gleaming bright

From afar, drawing near
Falls the night.

Thanks and praise for our days
'Neath the light, 'neath the moons, 'neath the sky
As we go, this we know
God is nigh.

THE LAST BYE

CHAPTER IX

Resume

After the ceremony there was a long time of talking between both Corlan and Tirran. P'erry had hoped that J'etsu's quirky accent and heavy-handed sense of humor would bring laughter to *C'lou*, and he was pleased to see her lay aside her grieving for a time. To him, her laughter was a wonderful thing to hear.

J'etsu told *C'lou* a slightly exaggerated and extremely humorous account of the events leading up to the day that P'erry flew on his back and of the flight itself. P'erry could not hear J'etsu's side of their conversation, but he knew exactly what story was being told, because when *C'lou* began to laugh so hard that she was nearly crying, she kept repeating the word *apparatus*. P'erry smiled.

When J'etsu got to the part of the story where P'erry's

unconscious body was banging against J'etsu's face and eyes, J'etsu began to demonstrate with his body, and *C'lou* laughed so hard she begged J'etsu to stop. By that point, P'erry was laughing at *C'lou's* laughter. *C'lou* found that letting herself laugh was like a medicine for her soul. It eased the pain of her suffering.

Late in the night, the non-winged people finally got into the longboats and went back to the ship to sleep. As they climbed into their bunks, thoughts began to turn to resuming the journey. How long would they stay on the island? How long would it take to reach the New Land?

The next morning, they all took care of the daily chores, and then rowed back to the island. Tap gathered Daniel, *Tess*, and P'erry to go inquire of the Tirra about the direction to the New Land. J'etsu approached them, and then he summoned Torreq for them.

When Torreq arrived, Daniel told him, "Shao was aided by your skill with the 'movable window.' You helped him to learn the right direction to get to the New Land. We need to learn all we can. We hope to learn not only the direction, but also the distance."

Torreq spoke to P'erry, who relayed, "Torreq says the Tirra will do all they can to help us."

Tess used a stick to draw a circle in the sand, and then she said, "Torreq, imagine that this circle represents Sset, our entire moon world."

Then she drew a line through the middle of the circle,

from left to right, splitting the circle into a top half and a bottom half. Finally she put a mark right in the middle of that equator line, dead center of the circle.

She continued, "Imagine that this line is the equator. Finally, imagine that we are here; that this mark in the very center is this island we're on now. Which way would we sail to reach the New Land?

P'erry knelt down and said, "Torreq says we would travel this way, directly along the equator." He gestured with his finger.

Tess then drew another circle, the same size. This time, she drew no equator line, and she put the mark for the island on the top edge of the circle.

She said, "Now imagine that I have changed our point of view to directly above the pole, and this mark is the island where we are now. Can you tell by using the movable window, how far around Sset we have to go before we reach the New Land?"

P'erry said, "Yes, it's—" and then he paused and looked back to Torreq. Torreq confirmed the answer, and P'erry again said, "Yes, it's here." He put his finger almost completely opposite of where the island was. The distance from them was more than a third of the circumference— about 80% of half the distance around the moon world.

Tess gasped, and then she said, "Torreq are you sure?"

After a moment, P'erry said, "Yes, he is sure."

Daniel said, "What is it? What's wrong?"

Tap said, "What does this mean?"

Tess said, "Well, it probably means that God has some kind of miracle planned. When I estimate the size of Sset based on the visual height of the horizon, which is very similar to Earth's, and also based on how strong the pull of gravity is here at the equator, which is also very similar to Earth's, I get a sense that Sset is about the same size as the Earth. These are not exact measurements, but I definitely get the sense that the two worlds are very close in size."

Tap said, "Go on."

Tess paused a long time, and then finally she said, "If this world is as big as the Earth, there is no natural way we can sail that far. Our ship is simply not big enough to carry enough food."

Tap sighed, and then he said, "If this means building a third ship—an even larger ship—then I and the other aging adults don't have enough life left in us to get there. We barely got this one built. I am showing more age with each passing week. Karq and Swov are even worse off than I am."

Everyone stood around, looking at the drawings in the sand and scratching their heads.

Daniel said, "Torreq, what if we sail the other way? Can we sail around the Old Land and then get to the New Land that way? Is that any shorter?"

P'erry listened and then said, "Torreq says no. He says

you could sail to the New Land that way, but it would take even longer."

Daniel posed, "What if Sset's core is made up of materials more dense than Earth's core? Wouldn't greater mass yield the same gravity while the planet's size would be smaller?"

Tess said, "Yes, but that fails to take into account my other test—the visual height of the horizon. If Sset were smaller and denser in mass, then the horizon would look low to us when compared to Earth, as though we were standing on a slightly mountainous incline. If Sset were larger and less dense in mass, then the horizon would look high to us when compared to Earth, as though we were standing inside a bowl-shaped valley. If Sset's core makeup were either more or less dense, we would either look up to the horizon, or down to the horizon, instead of over at the horizon."

Daniel nodded, "Right. I should know better than to question you on such things, but I'm just trying to figure out something."

Tap said, "What if we left the animals behind?"

Tess said, "I would strongly advise against that for two reasons. The first is that God guided Shao on selecting a partial list of all the kinds of animals. That means a couple of things. It means that taking the animals was God's idea, not Shao's. Therefore, disobeying is a bad idea.

"It also means that of all the animals that could have

161

been taken, God paired the list down. We have to remember that God knows which animals are necessary and which animals can be left behind. Perhaps the ones we left behind are already there and the ones we're bringing are not. Or, perhaps we're simply going to be able to get by with fewer kinds. Again, if God indicates these animals are to be taken, abandoning them is very unwise. Shao would not do it.

"The second reason is more base and practical, but still very compelling. As indicated by Torreq, the trip's distance is so far that we would not have enough food even if we removed every animal and replaced the newly emptied space with food."

Tap said, "Well, we need to call a meeting and discuss this."

Daniel said, "May I suggest we call a prayer meeting and discuss this with God."

Tess slowly said, "P'erry, God told Shao that you were the key; that you would be the one to figure out how to get us there. Shao said that you needed only to see the obvious." She pointed to the circles and said, "What do you see here? What are we missing?"

P'erry stared at the circles for a long time, and then he decided to simply risk being honest out loud. He had to push aside memories of being laughed to scorn.

He said, "I see bubbles, but they're not intersecting, and the straight line is in the wrong place."

"Bubbles?" Tap asked.

"Yes, sir."

P'erry stepped to the side of the original drawings, and made an illustration similar to the one drawn by Swov during school back on the Old Land.

He said, "This has to do with mass, but I'm not drawing Sset. I'm drawing two intersecting sedondi, and this is the *C'horat*, or in other words, *C'horat's* plane."

Tess encouraged him, "Son, I don't know where you're going with this, but it sounds interesting. Tell me, what is *C'horat's* plane?"

P'erry said, "Well, remember when I said that J'etsu cannot talk to me from a distance unless I am with someone? I think the reason is because when I am alone, there is no *C'horat's* plane. Whenever two sedondi intersect, the plane gets created. It is a place of balance, where there is no distortion of space-time by the two sedondi. Their distorting effects cancel each other out."

Tess smiled a proud-mom smile and said, "Do go on."

P'erry continued, "All bodies of mass have an invisible sedondi around them. It's a bubble-shaped distortion of space-time. This applies to creatures too. Celestial bodies can have sedondi that are really noticeable because of loose materials trapped in the gravity well, but the sedondi around people and animals are unnoticeable.

"*C'horat's* theory, which was nearly proved and has not been disproved, predicts that even with a certain amount of difference in mass between the two bodies, their plane of intersection will still be free of distortion.

"J'etsu told me his 'movable window' would not work inside my sedondi unless someone was near me. I think the movable window needs a *C'horat's* plane or else it cannot function. It needs a plane free from distortion."

P'erry looked at his parents and asked, "Didn't you say that back when you used to teleport on Earth, you opened a viewing portal on the 'far end' and moved it around—to see what was on the other side before you teleported? That sounds a lot like the Tirra's 'movable window.' What if teleportation *can* work here on Sset, but it just needs a *C'horat's* plane in order to function?"

Tap looked totally confused.

Daniel stood with his mouth open.

Tess' mind was moving so quickly based on what P'erry had suggested that she was too busy to even be proud of him. Eventually, she came back around. Then, she too stood with her mouth open—at first. Finally, a cautious smile appeared on her face.

She said, "P'erry, if this turns out to be doable, you will have saved everyone."

Tess then backed up, faced toward Daniel and tried to form a portal. She shook her head. Then she backed farther away and tried again. She again shook her head.

While she was trying, J'etsu said inside P'erry's mind, "I think you are right. Explain to them that I cannot talk

164

to you through the movable window if *either one of us* is alone. It just will not work. Also, you should point out that the larger the *C'horat*, the larger the window can be. The movable window can always be large whenever there are Tirra on both ends. I can never make it very big when there are only puny ones on your end."

P'erry quickly said, "Mom, try a really small portal. J'etsu says the size of the window is limited by the size of the *C'horat*. He also says that a *C'horat* is needed on both ends in order to open up a window that reaches *inside* of a sedondi on the other end."

Tess recalibrated and tried again. Suddenly she threw her hands into the air and shrieked with excitement.

"Yes!" she screamed. "It worked! I just opened up a tiny portal!"

Tap said, "What does this mean?"

"I'll show you," she said.

Tess used the *C'horat* between herself and Daniel as the near portal. She used the *C'horat* between P'erry and Tap as the far portal. Then she picked up a handful of wet sand from the beach, and tossed it toward Daniel's chest. Halfway there, it disappeared—simply vanished out of thin air—and at the same moment, it reappeared—again, right of thin air—between P'erry and Tap. The wet sand flew the rest of the way, and struck Tap on the arm.

Tap touched the wet sand, and then he smiled the biggest smile he had ever smiled.

"This is the most amazing thing I have ever seen!" he shouted.

Daniel literally began to dance. Oh, what a dance he danced!

Torreq chortled a huge sound that was half laugh, half roar. J'etsu fell over backwards, flipped a full roll, and sat back up on his hind legs. He made a gleeful squealing sound.

Daniel, *Tess*, and Tap all patted P'erry on the back.

Tess then said, "Let's see how big of a portal I can make." She tried quite a few more times at a variety of sizes. Then she wrinkled her brow and said, "The only problem I see is that the portals' maximum sizes are too small. I will need bigger *C'horats*."

Everyone simultaneously turned toward the two Tirra, as they all realized that since the Tirra weigh more, therefore they would be able to generate a larger *C'horat*.

Tess said, "Do you think I will be able to form an opening portal on a *C'horat* other than my own?"

P'erry grabbed the stick he had been using for drawing, and he modified his illustration. He added a smaller third sedondi, so the three were daisy-chained in a row.

He pointed to center of the smaller *C'horat* in the modified drawing and said, "Stand like this, Mom, and give it a try."

Tess positioned herself so that she, J'etsu, and Torreq were in a straight line with each other. She tried again.

"Yes!" she shrieked. "I just formed a huge portal. It's not big enough to get the ship through, but just about anything else would fit. I could even fit a Tirra through there."

She turned to P'erry and said, "Surf or sand?"

"Huh?" he replied.

"Walk that way, but tell me if you want to get wet or stay dry!"

Ever the adventurous one, P'erry said, "Wet!"

Then he ran past J'etsu and toward Torreq. When he reached the halfway point between the two Tirra, he vanished. In the same moment, he reappeared just over the surf, a couple of ment out from the land. He was still moving at full speed, yet he was running in mid-air over nothing.

"YIPPEEE!" P'erry shouted as he quickly soared downward and hit the water running.

J'etsu squealed, chortled, and rolled back and forth. He pounded the sand with his "knuckles" as he laughed.

Daniel yelled out, "J'etsu says he wants to do it! He wants to teleport!"

Tess replied, "In order for that to happen, I'm going to need—"

Before she could even finish her sentence, the beach near *Tess* and Daniel was suddenly covered with shadow, and then abruptly—WHOMPH! Two more Tirra landed near them.

Daniel said, "Torreq says he's way ahead of you."

"Well, I know that now!" Tess replied, "But I only needed one more Tirra!"

Daniel said, "Torreq says no, you need two more, because he wants to try it too!"

Tess suddenly asked, "Where is Tap?"

They all turned to see Tap literally running to tell the others.

"Look at him go!" Daniel said. "I thought he was too aged to move that fast."

"He's going to be paying for that jog in a little while," *Tess* said.

P'erry said, "Why didn't he just let you teleport him? He doesn't have the concept yet, does he?"

They all roared with laughter.

P'erry said, "Ooh, Mom! Teleport me to the others before he can get there!"

The rest of the Corlan were all talking together on the beach, near the landing site, when they saw Tap running toward them.

Tap said, "Oh, no! There must be something terribly wrong. I can't imagine what would make my husband run like that!"

As they all turned toward him, *Tap* started running to meet her husband.

Suddenly P'erry appeared before her, seemingly out of nowhere.

"Hello!" he greeted them all. "I just figured out how my parents can get us all to the New Land!"

Still some distance away, Tap saw P'erry appear, and he just stopped in his tracks.

He threw up his hands and yelled toward P'erry, "Very clever! Wish I'd thought of that!"

Then he sat down on the beach and began to laugh.

It took a very long time to explain the whole concept to everyone, but it was the most joyous school session in Corlan history. Swov grasped it first. Once he had the understanding, he just backed out and watched the bedlam as all those who grasped it tried to explain to all those who didn't.

Tess and Daniel, after several demonstrations and many efforts to explain, finally gave up and joined Swov.

They watched as P'erry tried yet again using drawings on the beach, still searching for the right way to explain.

Swov pointed to P'erry and said, "The student has become the teacher. I am a glorious success, I think. Wouldn't you agree?"

Daniel patted Swov on the back and said, "I do agree. You are a glorious success!"

Tess said, "So, you actually blew bubbles in class?"

Swov smiled and nodded as he said, "Yes."

Tess shook her head and said, "Thank God for creative teachers and for bubbles."

Swov turned to them and very seriously said, "And thank God for Daniel, *Tess*, and especially—P'erry."

When everyone felt like they grasped the concept, things finally calmed down.

C'lou became pensive, and she said to P'erry, "I wish my father could have seen this."

Tess heard her, and she said, "Me too, *C'lou*. Me too."

CHAPTER X

New Land, New Life

It was decided between Torreq, Tap, Daniel and *Tess*, that at least two Tirra would accompany the Corlan to the New Land, knowing full well that it was possible a contingency of Tirra might become a permanent resource on the far end of their pending journey. The reason was simple: Without Tirra there might be no way for any return trips. J'etsu volunteered to be one of the Tirra to visit the new land, and Torreq agreed to it. J'etsu and P'erry were ecstatic.

For *C'lou*, leaving was bittersweet because, while she longed to get to the New Land that her father had so desperately wanted for them all, she also hated to leave the place where he was buried.

Daniel saw *C'lou* staring up at the waterfall, and he

said, "It's hard to leave where he's buried, isn't it?"

"Yes, sir," she confessed. "I want to go, but part of me wants to stay."

Suddenly the thought occurred to Daniel that in the Bible, back on Earth, Joseph had insisted, prior to his death, that eventually his descendants were to carry his bones out of Egypt, whenever God finally rescued them and permitted them to go to the promised land.

Daniel went and found Tap and cited to him the passage (from Exodus 13:19): "Moses took the bones of Joseph with him because Joseph had made the sons of Israel swear an oath. He had said, 'God will surely come to your aid, and then you must carry my bones up with you from this place.'"

Tap thought for a moment and said, "Absolutely. If my father had ever known of or considered such an option, I am sure he would have wanted us to bury him in the New Land instead of here. The only ones I want to check with on this are *Shao*, *C'lou*, *Karq* and Torreq."

Later that same day, Tap caught up with Daniel and *Tess* as they were carrying in yet another load from the longboats. P'erry was with them.

Tap said, "Everyone thinks your idea is wonderful. It is agreed that when we all teleport to the New Land, we will fetch my father's body and take it with us. At some point soon afterward, we will prepare a burial site on the

New Land."

Tess was thrilled, and she said, "Great idea, Dan!"

Daniel said, "I can't take credit. The idea came from scripture. Now P'erry here, he's like you. He gets genius ideas out of his own creativity. Thank God."

With the help of the Tirra, unloading the ship was easier than loading it had been. However it was still a lot of work. It took two more days to get everything and every creature off the ship. Even the bunk frames were built to be portable, so they could be reused for beds on the far end of the journey.

Finally, they were all just about ready to make the jump. Every one was cautioned and then doubly cautioned about the danger of carrying any pollen through the "tele-portal" to the New Land. They prayed sincerely for God's help to find any and all pollen before making the trip. Then they checked every square inch of clothing, skin, hair, hide, fur, fruit, and supplies—you name it. Then they rechecked everything.

Daniel commented, "It's just like removing yeast before the Passover, when the Jews got ready to leave Egypt. And we're even going to be taking bones with us. I cannot get over it."

Tess said, "I hope it takes longer on Sset for a body to decompose, because back on Earth, Shao's corpse would *really* be stinking by now."

"We'll soon see," Daniel replied.

When it came time to make the jump, Torreq and two other Tirra went to get Shao's body. Everyone watched as a doorway was opened in the waterfall, and the Tirran Eldest landed and leaned into the cave. Then they watched as he flew toward them empty handed.

As Torreq landed, Swov announced, "Torreq says the cave is empty. The body is gone. Completely gone!"

Confusion abounded.

Suddenly Tap raised his hands and calmed everyone.

"This is the Lord's doing," he said. "I have confirmation from the Lord that this is His doing."

The most calm among them was *Shao*. She had a half smile on her face that hinted something wonderful.

At Tap's nod, *Tess* and Daniel each aligned themselves with their respective, appointed sets of Tirra for the necessary nearside *C'horats*. They each opened up a portal, and began "telesensing" (also called "televiewing"). When they finally had the two portals on the far end safely placed on the New Land, they announced they were ready for the departure to begin.

For a very long time, they all stayed on the nearside while continuously poking supplies and animals through the portals. Daniel and *Tess* kept adjusting the locations of the portals on the far side, so as to evenly distribute the supplies and animals.

Finally, it was time for the Corlan and Tirra to go. Tap, *Tap*, and *B'rei* went first. Next were Torreq, *Torreq*, and Torreq's daughter, *G'iza*, followed by J'etsu. Then *Shao* and *C'lou* went through.

On the far end, everyone appeared except *Shao*.

"What?" Daniel said.

"I see that," *Tess* said. "Everyone wait."

Swov said, "What is it?"

"*Shao* disappeared," Daniel said.

"Yes," Swov said, "We see that."

"You don't understand," *Tess* said, "She did not just disappear from here. She disappeared from anywhere. Everyone else came through on the far side except her."

"What?" Karq said, "The teleportation is not safe?"

"Just wait," *Tess* said, "Tap is saying something."

Daniel heard it more clearly, as Tap was closer to his portal on the far end.

"Tap says that this is the Lord's doing," Daniel said. "He said that he has confirmation from the Lord that this is His doing."

"I don't believe it," Karq said. "What have you done with our First Mother?"

Tess said, "We are telling you the truth, Karq. Tap is on the far end, standing on the New Land with the others. He is saying that the Lord is responsible for *Shao* not coming through."

"I don't believe it," Karq repeated. "This teleportation

is not safe. Bring our First Mother back at once!"

Daniel said, "If the Lord took her somewhere, how do you think we could get her and bring her here?"

Swov said, "Enough arguing. Everyone through the portal."

As everyone else moved toward the portal, Karq said, "*Karq*, as your husband I insist that you stay. T'anah, as your father I command you to stay. This teleportation is not safe. I don't trust it. I don't believe it. They could be killing us all."

Karq and T'anah stopped.

Swov said, "Enough of this! We are going now. We are *all* going, right now! Come on, Karq. Age and sickness are dulling your mind. Pray, seek counsel from God. You need not trust us. Trust the voice of God!"

"I don't believe in it," Karq said, apparently refusing to pray. "I will never believe in it. It is not safe. This is madness."

Swov shook his head and said, "Come on, *Swov*, R'ei, and *Z'aey*. Let's go."

As the four members of the Swov family moved toward the portal, *Z'aey* and T'anah looked at each other. If they got split up here, how would they ever be married in the New Land?

Z'aey called out, "T'anah, please."

T'anah bowed his head for a moment and prayed. He took the time to do that which his father refused to do.

Then he lifted his head and said, "Father, I am going. This is wrong. You are rebelling against the Lord, disobeying his will."

Karq said, "T'anah! How do you dare to disrespect your father so?! Be obedient!"

T'anah said, "Mother, God told our Eldest that P'erry was the key, that he would guide us to the New Land. This is the will of God. I sense this deep in my heart. This is right! What Father is saying is not! He is rebelling against the will of God. I cannot obey him in this!"

Karq said, "Son, we can still obey without going through the portal. We can get on the ship. We can stock it with enough food. With only our family on board, there will be enough food. We will still get to the New Land, just after a delay."

Karq looked at her son and pleaded with him, "Please, T'anah, stay with us. Surely God would not require of us a dangerous leap such as this. Listen to your father."

T'anah closed his eyes and prayed again for a moment.

When he opened his eyes, they were like the eyes of his grandfather, Shao. Eyes of unshakable determination.

"No," he said. "I am to always obey my parents in the will of God. I am not to follow them into rebellion against God. You doubt the very word of God."

With that, he turned to leave. He grasped *Z'aey's* hand, and went through the portal with the Swov family.

Daniel said, "Karq, I can tell you about some people back on Earth, a very long time ago, who doubted and refused to enter their New Land when God provided the way. Later they wished they had obeyed. Afterward, when they tried to enter at the wrong time, God did not allow them because of their doubt. They died in the wilderness. They never made it in.

"God kindly provided for them until their deaths, but they were never permitted to enter their New Land. If you refuse to come now, you will live out your few remaining days outside the New Land. You will never be permitted to enter. This is your last chance. Please."

Karq stood stock still, watching her husband's eyes. Somewhere, down deep inside her, she wanted to go, but the thought of living forever in the New Land without her husband made her willing to die with him outside it.

Karq raised his head in a proud stance and said, "Tele-portation is not safe. I do not believe in it. I am staying here. I will sail the ship by myself if I have to."

Tess said, "Suit yourself. P'erry, come on. Let's go."

Tess disconnected her portal, and then she and P'erry went together through Daniel's portal. Daniel could not go through his own portal, because the instant he would have stepped far enough into the sedondi of the Tirra, his sedondi would have become a "bubble within a bubble" and he would have a complete personal sedondi around himself, with no *C'horat* of his own with which to daisy chain a connection to the Tirran *C'horat*. Daniel waited patiently while Tess opened up a reverse connection from the other side. When he sensed the portal, he reached out to Karq one last time.

"Don't do this, Karq. Come with me. *Last chance.*"

Karq shook his head, and *Karq* hid her face—as though blocking Daniel from her sight would somehow remove her consciousness of her choice.

Daniel walked through the portal.

Everyone except *Shao* was waiting on the other side.

C'lou was in a total daze, and she anxiously watched the place where the portal had been, hoping her mother would somehow reappear. *Tess* and *Tap* stood by her side and encouraged her to have faith.

The rest of them all began to take in the New Land around them. It was a true paradise. They were situated on a flat plain near the ocean. It was covered with lush, healthy grass. Huge, beautiful trees could be seen not very far away. They saw many kinds of animals of various sizes in the air, on the ground, and in the trees. There were some kinds they had never seen before, and some they had seen before. Of the kinds they brought with them, none were seen.

They began to set up their tents, which would serve as homes until they could build houses.

Tap was bent over, attaching a tent line to a stake,

when, suddenly, he stopped and stood up.

"Wait," he said. "The Lord has said to me that we do not need to put up tents, or build houses."

"What?" his wife said.

Then, as if someone had tapped him on the shoulder, Tap turned. Then he pointed. They all turned.

Two figures approached them from the forest.

T'anah, who had excellent eyesight, said, "It's *Shao* and Shao!"

The two figures in the distance began to run toward them. They ran like youths. They ran for the fun of it.

C'lou led the way, as everyone ran to meet them. The gray-headed adults had to settle for a brisk walk.

Torreq and the other Tirra literally flew, and they reached them first. Torreq leaned his head down, and Shao hugged him. Next came *C'lou*. She wept for joy as she hugged both her parents.

As the others finally gathered close, they heard Shao laugh and say, "Torreq is offering for me to ride on his back, but I am telling him that he ought to ask me for a ride. I can now fly better than a Tirra."

He then turned his attention to all of them, and said, "You have done well! But where are Karq and *Karq?*"

Tap said, "Sire, regretfully we must report that Karq doubted God's word and His will, and he refused to come with us. He and his wife are still in the old land, on the first Tirran island."

Shao said, "I see. I feared that would happen. There was often something awry in his spirit. He has chosen his path. Sadly, they will die. His sin will be the death of his wife, but it will not destroy any of you who came."

He turned to T'anah and said, "You chose wisely. I am delighted in you, my grandson."

Shao said, "We are both now glorified immortals, like Daniel and *Tess*. Except... we don't have to worry about being limited by the *C'horat*. In fact, we can manipulate it and use it to great advantage."

Shao lifted his hands, and suddenly all the trees began to slide downward—or at least it looked that way at first. They all quickly realized that he had somehow lifted them into sky, even including the Tirra. He flew them all through the air, over the forest and around beautiful mountains.

While in their aerial journey, *Shao* said, "God has seen fit to provide wonderful homes for you. Shao and I both have stunning homes elsewhere, in a heavenly place, but we will be able to visit you as we wish. Where we now live, many of our children are there too—as glorified immortals like us. All those who died in faith during the plague are there. Some of them are coming to meet you."

Below them, in a picturesque valley, they began to notice beautiful homes arranged in a little hamlet. Shao lowered them to the ground in the midst of the new village.

Swov asked, "What about the animals we brought? And the supplies we left on the plain where we arrived?"

Shao smiled and said, "That is all being taken care of. The contaminated supply you brought along for a temporary food source is not needed. It is now gone. The uncontaminated seed was not truly needed, but there is no sense in letting it waste. It is now being sown in the plain. The animals you brought are doing fine. Welcome to a proper paradise."

At that instant, a crowd of glorified, immortal Corlan emerged out of nowhere and approached them from all sides. They were a mixture of long-lost children, parents, grandparents, aunts, uncles, cousins, nephews, and nieces. The hugging and laughter and joyful reunions went on and on.

Daniel and *Tess* went to Shao.

Tess said, "So you can manipulate the sedondi?"

"Yes, it is a very handy tool," Shao said.

Tess said, "About the *C'horat* theory—"

"It is not a complete understanding," Shao replied. "It is applicable in some respects, but not in others. However, it was enough to help you get here."

Tess said to Daniel, "It's probably like how Newtonian physics applies rather well on a massive scale, but it does not take Quantum physics into account. It is a helpful explanation, but an incomplete one."

Daniel told Shao, "You learned very quickly! You have

only been gone for a short time."

"I have been with the Lord. He is the great Teacher."

When they heard that, Daniel and *Tess* both looked at each other.

Tess said, "If He is still available, we would love to see him!"

"Certainly!" Shao said with a smile.

He teleported them both up to see the Lord.

Swov then approached Shao, and he asked, "Sire, will I recover from this terrible blight of age? Or will I eventually die here?"

"Come, my child," Shao said. He pointed to one of the opulent homes and said, "This one is for your family. The food here will wash away your age. You will live and not die. Inside here is a meal prepared that will get you started."

The two of them entered the impeccable new house. There a table was spread with delicious, uncontaminated food. They sat down together, but Swov's hunger for answers outweighed his desire for food.

Swov asked, "Sire, will I ever be granted a glorified body, such as you and *Shao* now have?"

"Yes, but God has ordained that such changes usually happen at the end of an age. He does make exceptions."

Swov asked, "What age are we in?"

"God tends to allow His people to pin names of their own choosing on the various ages. Call this one whatever you like. Perhaps 'The First Age of the New Land' or 'Second Golden Age.'"

"When will this age end?"

"I don't know. The Lord has not told me. The next big event I can foresee on the horizon is the death of P'erry. Or perhaps the Lord will spare him from death, and change him directly, as He did for *Shao*."

Swov said, "P'erry will surely marry and have children —perhaps many children. Will his children be able to have the memories passed to them? Will they be mortal, or immortal? Are the days of people being affected by the sin curse from Earth finally ended?"

"Now you are asking the most telling questions," Shao answered. "I'm told that his male descendants will not get the memories, but all the female descendants will. All his children will be mortal, but they will live very, very long lives compared to the earlier Humans of Earth. They will be vastly improved as well. Because of these surroundings and the infusion of Corlan genes, they will supersede the earlier Humans in nobility of spirit, mind, and body, although they will still be capable of sin, if corrupted— and in such cases the males will tend to do far worse and be more evil. Many among them will possess wonderful wisdom and profound discernment, and occasionally there will be prophets among them.

"They will coexist with the immortal Corlan, and, except for their limited lifespans and the lack of ancestral memories in the males, they will often be indistinguishable from the immortal Corlan. A few of his descendants will turn to darkness, but, thankfully, only a very few. During such times, it will take wisdom, strength, and valor on the part of his righteous descendants—as well as the immortal Corlan—to expel the evil from the land. We can help in such times. This world now has a place for the wicked: the Old Land. Be vigilant to not allow wickedness to take root here.

"Woe unto the man who shows judgment when God demands mercy, and woe unto the man who shows mercy when God demands judgment!"

The End

About the Chronicles:

Hi, I'm Doug Joseph, author of the Skyport Chronicles. I trust you enjoyed reading Book Three, and I encourage you to read all the books in the series, available (in both print and ebook editions) wherever books are sold. You can read free samples online at  SkyportChronicles.com. See the "Skyport Time Line" below to find where this book fits into the overall story arc. For the latest news on the series, see the publisher's website at WhiteStonePublishing.com, or to see what I'm up to, visit my blog at DougJoseph.net! By the way, as of the time of this publishing I am working on Book Four of the series! You're really going to love it!

Skyport Time Line:

New Immortal (Skyport Chronicles, Book One)

"Broadened my horizons...."
—David S. Norris, Ph.D.
Best-selling Author, Professor of Bible &
Theology, Urshan Graduate School of
Theology, St. Louis, MO

"Forget James Bond & Jason Bourne..."
—Roy H. Williams
New York Times Bestselling Author,
"Wizard of Ads," Founder & President
of Wizard Academy, Austin, TX

Daniel Talbot is a teleporting, spy-
chasing, miracle-working immortal
serving in the royal court of Jesus
during the Millennial Kingdom age.

YA Fiction | Christian | Futuristic | Sci-Fi | Prophecy

Tesseract (Skyport Chronicles, Book Two)

"...Sequel to *New Immortal*...will delight
young adult readers. Combining other-
worldly time travel with divine
revelation....caters to both faith and the
imagination, taking salvation into the
future and into the stars."
—ForeWord Reviews

"...Terrific! There's action, adventure,
romance, sci-fi, and it does not
contradict the Bible. I loved it. What a
great story. My teenage daughter loved
it, too! Highly recommended."
—Christina Li, BA, MA
Bestselling Author, Journalist, and
Inspirational Speaker

YA Fiction | Christian | Futuristic | Sci-Fi | Romance

Available wherever books are sold.

www.ingramcontent.com/pod-product-compliance
Lightning Source LLC
Chambersburg PA
CBHW022109170626
46808CB00002B/669